Raphael drew Jaime against his chest

Her jacket was unfastened, and his palms slid easily to her breasts. His hands lingered, but she lifted her hands to stop him. Raphael twisted her mouth to his, and beneath the sensual probing of his kiss, her objections were forgotten.

His kisses became deeper, more passionate, arousing her to a reluctant awareness of her own sexuality. When he lifted his mouth to seek the hollow at her nape, her fingers gripped the hair at the back of his neck as her lips sought a sensual consummation.

It was Raphael who eventually dragged himself away. "You see how it is between us?" he demanded. "Now tell me you don't want to see me again."

ANNE MATHER
is also the author of these

Harlequin Presents

and these
Harlequin Romances

Many of these books are available at your local bookseller.

For a free catalog listing all titles currently available,
send your name and address to:

HARLEQUIN READER SERVICE
1440 South Priest Drive, Tempe, AZ 85281
Canadian address: Stratford, Ontario N5A 6W2

ANNE MATHER

an elusive desire

Harlequin Books

TORONTO • NEW YORK • LOS ANGELES • LONDON
AMSTERDAM • PARIS • SYDNEY • HAMBURG
STOCKHOLM • ATHENS • TOKYO • MILAN

Harlequin Presents first edition April 1983
ISBN 0-373-10586-X

Original hardcover edition published in 1983
by Mills & Boon Limited

Printed in U.S.A.

CHAPTER ONE

JAIME was in a meeting when the call came through, and her secretary, Diane Stephens, was obviously very chary about disturbing her.

'It's a Signora di Vaggio, Miss Forster,' she explained, with evident reluctance. 'She says she's an old friend of yours, and it's imperative that she speaks with you.'

'Signora di Vaggio?' With the participants at the meeting waiting impatiently for her to deal with the interruption and return to their discussions, Jaime's mind was briefly blank. She didn't know anyone called *Signora* di Vaggio. Diane must have got it wrong. 'I'm afraid——'

'She sounds very upset, Miss Forster.' Diane lowered her voice perceptibly. 'I wouldn't have troubled you, but I think you ought to take the call. She says she wrote to you and——'

'*Nicola!*' The name broke from Jaime's lips as comprehension of what Diane was saying brought a swift understanding. Nicola di Vaggio! She was so used to thinking of her as Nicola Temple, even the use of Rafaello's name had not immediately registered. After all, it was more than five years since she had heard from her, and the letter which had arrived a week ago was still largely unread.

'You will speak to her, Miss Forster?'

Diane was gazing anxiously at her, and aware of the

growing impatience of her colleagues, Jaime was tempted to refuse. But if Nicola had put a call through from Italy, something serious must be wrong, and in deference to the friendship they had once shared, Jaime rose to her feet.

'If you'll excuse me for a few moments, gentlemen,' she offered apologetically, and ignoring Graham Aiken's pointed stare, she followed Diane out of the room.

Her office was just along the corridor, next door to Martin Longman's, the managing director of Helena Holt Cosmetics. It was the obvious place for the office of his personal assistant to be, and Jaime had fought hard to gain her present position.

'I'm sorry, Miss Forster,' said Diane, as Jaime shortened her stride to fit that of her secretary. 'But she sounded so distressed, I didn't know what to do.'

'That's all right, Diane.' Jaime smiled to reassure her. 'You were right to tell me. Signora di Vaggio and I are old friends.'

Diane looked relieved, and when they reached her office she slipped efficiently into her seat, preparing to switch the call through to Jaime's inner sanctum. With the door closed behind her, Jaime crossed her office with a sudden ripple of apprehension, lifting the cream receiver cautiously before acknowledging her presence.

'Jaime? Jaime, is that you? Oh, thank heavens!' The voice at the other end of the line held a distinctly hysterical note. 'Why didn't you answer my letter? Why are you never at home when I phone? I've been trying to reach you for days!'

'Nicola? Nicola, calm down.' Jaime was disturbed

by the hysteria in the other girl's voice. 'I'm here now—you're speaking to me. What can be so desperate that you found it necessary to ring me at work?'

'At work!' Nicola's voice sounded suspiciously near to breaking. 'When are you ever anywhere else? I've phoned your apartment four times, and every time that damn housekeeper of yours has answered.'

'Mrs Purdom?' Jaime frowned. 'So it's you who's been calling. Why didn't you give your name? Mrs Purdom was becoming convinced a gang of thieves was planning a robbery, and you were phoning to find out if I was home.'

'Oh, Jaime!' Nicola sniffed. 'I couldn't give my name—I didn't want you phoning here and speaking to Raf.'

'Really?' Jaime's fingers tightened round the receiver.

'Oh, not because of that.' Nicola made an impatient sound. 'I've got over all that. It's just—well, I don't want him to know I've called you. At least, not until it's necessary.'

'Nicola, what are you talking about?' Jaime could hear a certain tightness in her voice, but she couldn't help it. Five years was not such a long time, after all, and some things simply couldn't be forgotten.

'I want you to come and stay,' said Nicola, without preamble. 'Please, Jaime——' this as her friend started to speak, 'don't say no. Not until you've heard my reasons, anyway. I need someone so desperately, and there's no one else I can talk to.'

'Nicola, it's impossible——'

'Why is it impossible?' Nicola spoke urgently.

'Jaime, you don't understand. I'm almost going out of my head here. I *need* you, don't you understand, I need you. You can't just say no without listening to what I have to say.'

Jaime sighed. 'Nicola, if something's gone wrong with your marriage——'

'If something's gone wrong!' Nicola uttered a bitter cry. 'Jaime, everything's gone wrong, but everything. That's why I want you to come out here. That's why I need to talk to you. If I don't talk to someone soon I'll—I'll go mad!'

'Nicola, your mother——'

'You know Mummy and I never could talk to one another.'

'Your father, then.'

'Oh, Daddy!' Nicola was scornful. 'He's so wrapped up in the bank, he hardly ever notices I exist!'

'That's not true, Nicola. You know he'd do anything to make you happy——'

'So long as whatever I want can be bought and paid for,' exclaimed Nicola unsteadily. 'Jaime, you know what Daddy's like. He thinks money can buy anything.'

'It can buy most things,' put in Jaime tautly. 'Nicola, whatever you say, I don't think I'm the person you need to talk to. Whatever it is, why can't you talk it over with Rafaello——'

'Raf!' Nicola choked on his name. 'No, I can't talk it over with Raf. He won't even talk about it,' she declared confusingly. 'Jaime, please—*please*! I know we haven't seen one another for a long time, and I know you were unhappy when I married Raf, but—that's all in the past now. Surely you can forgive me——'

'There was nothing to forgive, Nicola,' replied Jaime stiffly. 'You must have known——'

'I know we never talked about it, but—well——' Nicola hesitated. 'It can't have been easy for you when Raf made me his wife.'

Jaime held herself tightly in control. She would not get involved in an argument over Rafaello di Vaggio, *she would not*. Like Nicola said, it was all in the past now. Even admitting her aversion to getting involved in Nicola's problems was to invite the suspicion that she still nurtured some resentment over what had happened; and she didn't; she *couldn't*.

'Look, Nicky,' she said, using her old pet name for her deliberately, 'I'm right in the middle of a meeting with a group of sales representatives, and I really don't have the time for this now. Can I call you back?'

'No.' Nicola spoke quickly. 'I mean—I'll call you back. Just tell me when and where, and I'll manage it somehow.'

Jaime hesitated. 'This evening, then, at the apartment. Say about six-thirty.'

'Your time or mine?'

'It's summertime. They're both the same,' replied Jaime shortly, and rang off before Nicola could say any more.

It was difficult returning to the meeting. It was difficult trying to pick up the threads of the discussion she had been having with the sales force, particularly as she knew half of them resented her being there in the first place. But Martin Longman had chosen her out of an estimated one hundred applicants, and his confidence in her ability to handle the job more than made up for the petty jealousies she sensed from her more chauvinistic contemporaries. She knew many of them believed that her appointment owed more to her appearance than to her professionalism, but Jaime had learned to ride the insults that were frequently tossed her way.

'I suggest we continue this meeting after lunch, gentlemen,' she said, after re-establishing her position as chair-person. 'I think we all need a little time to think over the proposals that have been made, and if anyone has any particular point they'd like to make, perhaps they would contact Miss Stephens and she'll arrange a suitable schedule for this afternoon.'

'You will be joining us, won't you, Jaime?' enquired Graham Aiken, with veiled sarcasm. 'Or perhaps you have more pressing matters to attend to.'

Jaime's smile was a triumph of self-possession. 'Oh, yes, I'll be joining you, Graham,' she declared smoothly. 'I have one or two points to put forward myself, and as Mr Longman's representative I shall expect full reports from all of you concerning the sales figures for your particular areas.'

Graham's lips thinned. 'Then I trust we won't spend half the afternoon waiting while you waste the firm's time taking personal calls,' he retorted offensively.

'Oh, come off it, Aiken!' Harold Ingram, one of the older representatives, slapped the other man on the back. 'You're only jealous because our beautiful assistant to the managing director doesn't take any personal calls from you.'

'Perhaps he's hoping to divert attention from the fact that sales in the south-east have been falling recently,' put in Hywel Evans sagely. 'What's the matter, Aiken? Losing your touch?'

The slightly edged banter continued as they all left the meeting, and although Jaime was grateful that for once she seemed to have come out best in the argument, her thoughts were too absorbed with the conversation she had had with Nicola di Vaggio to enjoy it. She couldn't imagine what could have gone wrong with Nicola's marriage to warrant that strange invitation, and while her natural curiosity was aroused, so too was a troubled sense of foreboding. They had not corresponded, they had not kept in touch after Nicola's precipitate marriage to the wealthy Italian count, whose title she now seemed to have abandoned. Why then should Nicola contact her now, when the most logical people she should confide in were her own mother and father?

In her office, Jaime seated herself at her desk and observed the neat stack of letters Diane had left for her perusal. But she didn't examine the letters. She didn't even look at them. Instead, she surveyed the room in which she was sitting, appreciating anew the undiminishing feeling of satisfaction it gave her.

It was a beautiful office, light and spacious, with wide, double-glazed windows overlooking the muted roar of London's busy streets twenty floors below. The walls were panelled in mahogany, reaching up to a high moulded ceiling that added to the room's airiness, and the floor was snugly fitted with a dark red carpet. There was a light oak desk, several comfortable leather armchairs, a shelf of books illustrating the different kinds of cosmetics used throughout the ages, and an exquisitely carved cabinet, which served both as an ornament and as a handy container for the refrigerated cupboard that held refreshments for visitors. It was the office of someone of importance, an executive, at least, and Jaime never ceased to marvel at her own good fortune in owning it.

She sighed now, leaning back in her seat and allowing her shoulders to rest against the cool dark leather. But she kept her hands on the desk, as if afraid it might suddenly disappear in this sudden, and unwelcome, rush of memory. Against the cloth, the silvery brilliance of her hair was etched in stark relief, the plain gold earrings that hung from her lobes her only ornamentation. Her suit, a simple design in dark green linen, accentuated the tall slender lines of her figure, but even its severe cut could not disguise the undoubted proof of her femininity. In spite of her determination to compete on equal terms in a man's world, she was still essentially female, and it was that awareness now that brought the troubled crease to her brow. What was Nicola up to? Why had she brought her problems to Jaime? And more importantly, how was Jaime going to get out of that unwanted invitation?

A tap at her door brought her head up with a start, and she smiled with some relief when she met her secretary's anxious eyes.

'I'm going to lunch now, Miss Forster,' Diane said diffidently. 'Is there anything I can get you before I leave?'

'Oh—no, thank you, Diane.' Jaime shook her head. 'I'll just have a sandwich here.' Her nail nudged the pile of untouched mail. 'I'll get around to some of these later.'

'Very well, Miss Forster.' Diane was only nineteen and still slightly in awe of her new boss. 'There's nothing urgent. Oh—but Mr Longman called. He said to tell you, he'd be in to the office tomorrow morning.'

'Fine.' Jaime swung her chair back and forth in a semi-circular motion. 'I guess I can handle anything that comes up. You go and get your lunch, Diane. I may need you to work over this evening.'

'This evening?' Consternation showed in the girl's face, and Jaime moved forward in the chair to rest her elbows on the desk.

'You've got a problem?'

'I've got a date,' admitted Diane reluctantly. 'But I could break it . . .'

'You don't want to, is that it?' Jaime gave her an understanding look. 'Okay, Diane, you keep your date. If necessary, you can work over lunch tomorrow, hmm?'

'Oh, thanks, Miss Forster!' Diane's gratitude was fervent. 'See you later, then.'

'Later,' agreed Jaime, nodding her head, and as Diane left the room, she rose to her feet to walk across to the window.

It seemed a long time since she had been like Diane, she reflected ruefully, and then grimaced. It was a long time—almost eight years, to be exact. She had been eighteen when she started to work for Helena Holt Cosmetics, but unlike Diane, she had made her work the whole centre of her existence.

From the very first day, she had been ambitious. Before that—from the time she and her mother had been struggling to keep their heads above water and a cousin of her mother's had taken pity on her and sent her to a decent school, she had been determined to make a success of her life. Her parents had divorced when she was very young, and as soon as Jaime was off her hands, her mother had retired to the country, to become companion to some elderly spinster. Jaime hadn't seen her father for years, not since she was at junior school, and the years spent at an exclusive girls' boarding school had taught her to be self-sufficient.

It had not always been easy. When she first started work, she had to live in dingy rooms and bedsitters, walking to work across town, and eating in cheap snack bars. Every spare penny she had, she had saved, and with it she had paid for an evening course at a commercial college, where she could supplement her knowledge of shorthand and typing with other skills like accountancy and economics. She had been an apt pupil, and when a vacancy had occurred in the progress office, she had applied. Much to the chagrin of some of the male applicants, she was successful, and she left the typing pool for the greener fields of advertising and finance. And yet, even then, she had not been content . . .

Turning from the window now, Jaime wondered, not for the first time, how much of her success was due to the way she looked. Certainly, her boss in the progress office, Clifford Jacobs, had found her very attractive—so much so that Jaime had had to fend off the accusations of his wife when she came storming into the office one evening to find Jaime and her husband closeted in his office discussing a new promotion. Not that there had been anything for Rebecca Jacobs to get so uptight about. Jaime wasn't interested in men, she wasn't interested in sexual relationships; and although her contemporaries might find that hard to believe from her appearance, they soon discovered her reputation was not misplaced. Only one man had succeeded in exploiting the weaknesses she had always subdued, and she had dealt with him as ruthlessly as her father had dealt with her mother. No man was going to control her. No man was going to make her dependent on him, financially or emotionally. There was only one way she knew for a woman to make her own way in the world, and that was by remaining free and unattached—and capable of providing herself with the kind of lifestyle men set so much store by.

It was late when she got home that evening, later than she had expected, due to Diane's early departure, and Mrs Purdom met her at the door with the news that 'that woman' had called again.

Jaime sighed, glancing at her watch to discover it was almost a quarter to seven, and nodded. 'I know, Mrs Purdom,' she said, surprising the elderly housekeeper with this knowledge. 'She called me at work today. It's someone I used to—go to school with.'

'Well, really!' Mrs Purdom was not appeased, and as she helped Jaime off with her jacket she showed her disapproval. 'Why couldn't she tell me who she was, instead of refusing to give her name? If you're old friends . . .'

'She doesn't want her husband to know she's been calling me,' replied Jaime drily, smiling at Mrs Purdom's disbelieving expression. 'It's true. Wasn't there ever a time when you kept something from your husband, Mrs Purdom? Didn't you have any secrets you wanted to hide?'

'Not that I can think of,' retorted Mrs Purdom with indignation, and Jaime kicked off her shoes as she walked into her living room.

'Well, lucky you,' she remarked, dropping her briefcase on to the couch and approaching the drinks tray Mrs Purdom had left ready for her. 'However, it does go to prove how confining that kind of a relationship can be.'

'If you want to make it so,' replied Mrs Purdom, watching with some misgivings as Jaime helped herself to a gin and tonic. 'Well, and what time will you be wanting dinner? It's a cold meal, so you can please yourself.'

Jaime lounged gracefully on to the couch, curling one of her long legs beneath her. 'Oh, in about an hour, thank you, Mrs Purdom,' she answered, putting up a lazy hand to loosen the coil of hair secured at her nape. 'I think I'll take a bath before I eat. I'm tired, I may have an early night.'

Mrs Purdom's somewhat severe features softened. With her hair loose and falling in straight lines about her face, Jaime looked years younger than the elegant business executive who had walked into the apartment, and the housekeeper regarded her anxiously. With her guard down, and the strain of the afternoon's business meeting showing in her face, Mrs Purdom thought she seemed more weary than usual, and the affection she felt for her employer kindled as she bent to gather up Jaime's shoes.

'You look tired,' she declared, holding the shoes against her, and Jaime sighed.

'Thanks!'

'No, you know what I mean,' exclaimed the

housekeeper warmly. 'You need a holiday, Miss Forster. You didn't have one last year, and it's already the end of May and you've made no plans for taking one this year either. What you need is a couple of weeks in the sun, away from dusty offices and boardrooms. Mr Longman would let you go, whenever you liked— you know he would. Doesn't sunbathing on some hot sunny beach appeal to you?'

'Not particularly.' Jaime gave the housekeeper a rueful smile. 'I'm not the lotus-eating kind, Mrs Purdom. Besides, we're launching the new range in three weeks, and I can't be away for that. It's my baby.'

'If you ask me, you'd be better employed having a real baby, instead of a cosmetic one!' retorted Mrs Purdom shortly, and Jaime gurgled with laughter.

'A cosmetic one! That's good, Mrs Purdom. I must remember that. I may be able to use it in our next promotion.'

The elderly housekeeper sighed. 'You won't be serious, will you?'

'About having a baby? No.' Jaime gave her an old-fashioned look. 'I'm not married, Mrs Purdom.'

'Nor likely to be, judging by the way you behave,' exclaimed the housekeeper dourly. 'What happened to that nice Mr Penfold? You had him here to dinner a couple of times, and I thought——'

'Robert Penfold is just a good friend, Mrs Purdom,' replied Jaime firmly, finishing her drink and placing the glass on the low table beside the couch. She rose lithely to her feet. 'I think I'll have my bath now. I'll let you know when I'm ready to eat.'

Mrs Purdom shrugged expressively, but she said no more, and Jaime was grateful. Right now, she was in no mood to argue her reasons for not seeing Robert Penfold any more, and the prospect of a long soak in a hot bath was much more to her liking. There was still the problem of what she was going to do about Nicola's call, and she hoped that a period of relaxation might provide her with sudden illumination.

Leaving the living room, Jaime crossed the narrow hall that separated it from her bedroom. In the beige and gold apartment she had decorated herself, she shed the rest of her clothes with some relief, and walked with feline grace into the adjoining bathroom.

As the water hissed and spurted into the sunken tub, she reflected, as she had done many times since she acquired this apartment two years ago, how lucky she was to have such pleasant surroundings to come home to. The last flat she had had, which had certainly been an improvement on the bedsitters she had previously occupied, had not been much bigger than her living room here, with a tiny bedroom and kitchen, and a bathroom that did not contain a bath, only a shower. One of the first things she had done when she leased this apartment was to spend part of every evening in the tub, luxuriating in its depth and size, and the sybaritic sensuality of the water.

As well as her bedroom and bathroom, there was a second bedroom and bathroom which Mrs Purdom used, the living room, of course, and a dining room and kitchen, fitted with every modern gadget available. There was even a small study, where Jaime could work in private, and situated as the apartment was on the tenth floor of the building, it was not troubled by the traffic sounds from Elgin Square.

She was just lifting her foot to step into the steaming water when the telephone started to ring. Frustrated at the realisation that she had not yet had time to think about what she was going to do, Jaime was tempted not to answer it, but something, some inner sense of loyalty perhaps to the girl Nicola had been, made her reach for a fluffy lemon bathrobe.

She reached the bedroom phone just as her housekeeper lifted the kitchen extension, and picking up the receiver, she said: 'I'm here, Mrs Purdom.'

'It's me, Jaime, not Mrs Purdom,' exclaimed Nicola's voice huskily, and Jaime heard the housekeeper ring off as she explained the situation.

'I'm sorry I missed your call earlier,' she added, perching on the edge of the bed. 'I'm afraid I was late getting home from the office. My secretary had to leave early, and there were one or two things I wanted typed up, so I did them myself.'

'My, how efficient you sound,' remarked Nicola, rather caustically. 'The perfect lady executive! What's it like to be able to boss people around, Jaime? Your secretary told me you're Martin Longman's assistant now. You certainly have made a success of your career.'

Jaime breathed deeply. 'Is that why you rang, Nicola? To talk about my job? Because I should tell you, I have a hot bath waiting, and a pile of contracts to go over after dinner.'

'Damn it, Jaime, don't be so bloody supercilious!' Nicola's voice broke on a sob. 'You know why I'm ringing, why I've been ringing for the past week or more!' She paused. 'Have you thought over what I asked you? Or—or is all this talk about how busy you are intended to warn me you haven't the time to consider my invitation?'

Jaime sighed. 'Nicola, whatever you want to talk to me about, couldn't you tell me now? Or write me a letter? I promise I'll reply as——'

'No! No, I couldn't.' Nicola's voice rose perceptibly. 'I need to see you, Jaime. I need to talk to you face to face. As—as for telling you over the phone——' She broke off and then continued in a lower key: 'Anyone could be listening, anyone. Raf has spies everywhere, I know he has. He doesn't trust me, you see. He never has. Oh, Jaime, please say you'll come out here. If—if you don't, I may just—just kill myself!'

CHAPTER TWO

OF course she wouldn't! Jaime knew that. Or at least, that was what she told herself as the British Airways Boeing flew smoothly south over the snow-capped peaks of the Swiss Alps thousands of feet below her. People who threatened suicide seldom actually went through with it. It was a cry for help, that was all; the only means Nicola could think of to get her to do what she wanted. All the same, it was a request Jaime had found herself unable to refuse.

Even so, as she made arrangements to take two weeks' leave of absence from her job, Jaime had known herself for a fool. It was the wrong time to be vacating her desk; it was the wrong place for her to be going; and it was certainly for the wrong reasons that she was setting out on such a mission. On top of everything else was the certain knowledge that Rafaello would not welcome her to the Castello di Vaggio, and she doubted very much whether Nicola had even told him that she was coming.

Her boss, Martin Longman, had been disappointed but understanding. 'If you really think this friend of yours is in danger of losing her mind, then of course you must go,' he said, when she first broached the subject with him. 'But remember, the launch of Lady-Free takes place three weeks from Friday. I expect you to be back before then.'

'Oh, I shall be.' Jaime was determined, gripping the

arms of her chair tightly as she sat across the desk from the man who was responsible for giving her this wonderful opportunity. 'I've checked with Clifford Jacobs, and with the manufacturers, and everything's going according to schedule. Unless there are any unforeseen problems, we should make it as arranged.'

'I hope you're right.' Martin Longman lay back in his chair, regarding his personal assistant with faintly troubled eyes. It had been his decision to promote a woman to the position previously always occupied by a man, and so far he had had no cause for complaint. Jaime had accomplished her duties with efficiency and precision, bringing to the job a flair that her predecessors had lacked. Perhaps a woman was the logical choice, after all, Martin reflected, reaching for the box of cigars that was never far from his elbow. To listen to his board one would never have thought so, but even the most prejudiced among them had been forced to acknowledge that Jaime Forster had acquitted herself with skill and enthusiasm.

Jaime, watching the fleeting expressions crossing her boss's face, knew a momentary anxiety. What did Martin really think of her asking for time off now with this important launch in the offing? Was he asking himself whether a male executive would have committed so unprofessional an offence? Or was he prepared to give her the benefit of the doubt? In the past, she had never let him down. Did he think she was letting him down now?

'If you feel I shouldn't be away at this time——' she began, but she didn't get to finish her statement.

'I know you wouldn't have asked, if it hadn't been a matter of life and death,' remarked Martin wryly.

'Come along, I'll buy you lunch. That will give the hawks in the boardroom something else to worry about!'

Jaime's smile was grateful as they went down in the lift. It wasn't the first time Martin had bought her lunch, and she knew that fact was frequently seized upon by her opponents in their efforts to get her abilities disparaged. But her friendship with the managing director remained on a purely business footing, even though she knew he had marital problems of his own.

They went to the Highwayman, a hotel within walking distance of the offices in Holland Park. They went straight into the restaurant, and after the meal was ordered and pre-lunch drinks had been brought, Martin regarded her thoughtfully over the rim of his glass.

'Who is this friend of yours?' he enquired, his bushy brows drawing together interrogatively. 'You've spoken of your friends before, but I don't remember a Nicola being mentioned. How long have you known her?'

'Since schooldays.' Jaime sipped her Martini appreciatively. 'Nicola was in my year at Abbotsford. We were quite—close friends.'

'Are,' corrected Martin drily, putting his glass aside. 'Or was that a Freudian slip?'

Jaime gave a short laugh. 'Perhaps. I haven't seen Nicola for more than five years. Not since—not since she got married, in fact.'

'Ah.' Martin was looking intrigued. 'Do I detect a thwarted romance?'

'No.' Jaime was delighted to discover she could speak quite calmly. 'But—well, she married an Italian.

A count, actually. The Conte di Vaggio. He took her back to Tuscany, and we just lost touch with one another.'

'Yet she knew where to find you,' Martin pointed out, and Jaime nodded.

'I was already working for Holts when she left England. Just because I'm no longer in the typing pool it doesn't mean the receptionist wouldn't know where to find me.'

'I suppose not.' Martin looked at her humorously. 'I wonder how you are regarded in the typing pool now. To travel so far in such a short time!'

'Do you regret it?'

Jaime's thickly-lashed grey eyes invited his opinion, and Martin shook his head. A handsome man, still only in his middle fifties, he attracted a lot of female attention, and they both knew that their relationship was the source of constant speculation throughout the company. But now he simply reached out and covered one of her hands with his, and said quietly:

'You're the best assistant I've ever had, and you know it. Just don't get to thinking you might like to try the matrimonial state yourself while you're out there. Italians are very keen on the family, I know, and if your friend's husband has any eligible brothers or cousins or uncles desirous of a wife, remember you've got a professional family here, depending on you.'

Jaime smiled. 'I'll remember.'

'Good.' Martin nodded approvingly. 'Ah, here comes our smoked salmon. Let's enjoy the food and talk about this new idea I have for promoting our products alongside a matching range of garments. I mean, if we could create a certain image, a Helena Holt look . . .'

Jaime looked down at the screen of cloud cover which had emerged to hide the blue waters of the Mediterranean far below them. That lunch with Martin had taken place two days ago, two days in which she had been rushed off her feet, clearing up all outstanding matters at the office and finding time in her lunch hour to shop for one or two shirts and sweaters, suitable for early June in that north-western part of Italy known as Tuscany.

Mrs Purdom had been a boon, laundering and pressing and packing her suitcase with all the items necessary for a week-long stay at the Castello di Vaggio. Jaime had limited her agreement to accept Nicola's invitation to one week only, allowing herself the other week in case anything should go wrong. She didn't know what could go wrong, but Nicola had never been a particularly stable character, and although Jaime suspected she had exaggerated the situation, her hysteria on the phone last evening had not been pretence.

Mrs Purdom, on the other hand, persisted in regarding the trip as a holiday. She was the only one, apart from Nicola, of course, who welcomed Jaime's enforced holiday.

'I said you needed a break,' she had declared smugly, as she prepared Jaime's breakfast that morning. 'A week or two in Italy will make all the difference to you—get you out of that office, and put some colour in your cheeks.'

'It's not a pleasure trip, Mrs Purdom.' Jaime was

half impatient. 'I'm just helping out an old friend, that's all. I'll be back, I hope by the middle of next week.'

'Well, don't you hurry. There's nothing spoiling here,' declared Mrs Purdom irrepressibly. 'Now, are you sure there's nothing you've forgotten before I lock your case?'

'Ladies and gentlemen, the No Smoking sign has now been switched on, and passengers are requested to check that their seat belts are fastened, that chairs are in the upright position, and that all cigarettes are extinguished. No smoking is allowed until passengers are inside the terminal buildings. We shall be landing at Pisa airport in only a few minutes. Thank you.'

The stewardess smiled at Jaime as she put her microphone away and Jaime felt the familiar sense of tension she always experienced prior to landing. It wasn't anticipation of the landing itself. She had flown to Paris and Rome several times during her years at Helena Holt, and only two months ago, Martin had taken her with him on a trip to New York. It was the uneasy touch of apprehension she felt upon arriving at an alien destination, and in this instance she felt doubly apprehensive at the knowledge that within a couple of hours she would be meeting Rafaello again.

The aircraft landed without incident, and as Jaime was sitting at the front of the plane, she was one of the first to disembark. She passed through Passport Control without a hitch, collected her suitcase from the unloading bay, and then walked swiftly through Customs, keeping an alert eye open for Nicola's diminutive figure.

The arrivals lounge was full of people waiting for

friends and relations to appear from any one of the half dozen aircraft that had landed since Jaime's flight touched down. Surely Nicola would have the sense to move to the front, thought Jaime tensely. Among so many taller people, she could easily be overlooked.

'Miss Forster!'

The crisp masculine tones set Jaime's nerves jumping. In spite of the fact that she had been steeling herself for this moment ever since she had agreed to Nicola's blackmail, she was alarmed to find that Rafaello's voice still had the power to turn her bones to jelly. She swung round, the suitcase dropping nervelessly from her hand, and confronted the man she had last seen, standing with his back to her, in the medieval beauty of Westminster Cathedral.

'Rafaello-Raf!' she stammered, despising herself for her incompetence. 'What a surprise! Where's Nicola? I thought she was coming to meet me.'

'Nicola's not well.' Rafaello's chilling dark eyes swept her anxious face without compassion. If she had changed, if *Nicola* had changed, Rafaello had not, and her tongue clove to the roof of her mouth as she surveyed his lean features.

He had always been tall, taller than the average Italian, and therefore topping her five feet eight inches by some four inches more. He was dark, as was to be expected, though not so dark that it was not possible to glimpse lighter strands in his dark hair. His skin was brown, textured by the sun, and the eyes that were surveying her so coldly were as black as hell's kettles.

'Nicola's ill?' For the moment Jaime tried to concentrate on what he was saying, not on the manner in which he was saying it.

'I said—not well,' Rafaello amended shortly. He picked up her suitcase. 'Is this all your luggage?'

'I—yes.' Jaime didn't like being disconcerted, but she was disconcerted now. 'I'm sorry you've been put to this trouble. If I'd known——'

'Yes? What would you have done?' Rafaello prompted, starting off across the crowded reception area. 'Put off your visit, perhaps? Given us a little more time to prepare for you?'

Jaime pressed her lips together as she followed him. With his leather-jacketed figure forging ahead of her, it was difficult to think coherently about anything. What was he implying? That she had invited herself to the Castello? It was obvious he didn't want her here, and truthfully she could hardly blame him.

Outside the airport buildings, the afternoon sun was infinitely warmer than its English counterpart. When she had left Heathrow, her cream flannel pants suit had not been out of place, but here in Italy, the trousers felt incredibly warm, and she shed her jacket to reveal the bronze silk shirt she had bought in Selfridges just last week. There was a breeze, however, and she was glad of its coolness against her cheeks, even if its errant current brought strands of silky hair to brush against her neck.

'If you will wait here, I will bring the automobile,' said Rafaello, pausing at the kerb and setting down her case. His dark eyes raked her flushed cheeks and tumbled hair before moving lower to denounce the unbuttoned neckline of her shirt. His scornful appraisal made her want to put up her hand and fasten the neck of her shirt, but she refused to succumb to so obvious a condemnation. Instead, she faced him proudly, uncaring that the wind was exposing the smooth curve of her breast, and with a silent imprecation, he strode abruptly away.

In Italy, all men enjoy looking at a beautiful woman, and in the five minutes or so before Rafaello returned with the car, Jaime quickly got used to countering their amorous glances. Even so, she was immensely relieved when Rafaello did return. She would not have been entirely surprised if he had chosen to abandon her after all.

The car, a sleek red Maserati, nosed to the kerb beside her, and Rafaello sprang out to stow her suitcase in the boot. 'Get in,' he directed, swinging open the door, and with a gesture of acquiescence Jaime obeyed. She noticed that when Rafaello came to join her, he made sure his thigh did not brush hers as he levered himself behind the wheel, and the car moved away smoothly, without any further need for conversation.

For a time, Jaime was content to remain silent. Indeed, Rafaello's attitude was such that she was tempted to let him nurture his ill-humour all the way to Vaggio. But concern for Nicola, and the awareness that for seven days, at least, she was expecting to enjoy his hospitality, inevitably aroused her own feelings of compassion. Even so, she waited until the hilly suburbs of the city were behind them, but once they were on to the anonymous *autostrada*, that connected Pisa with Florence, Jaime endeavoured to recover the situation.

'I assume you know that Nicola rang me,' she ventured, wishing for once that she smoked so that she had something to do with her hands, and then flinched when his lean face turned aggressively in her direction.

'*She* rang *you*?' he stated disbelievingly. 'You expect me to believe that?'

Jaime gasped. 'It's the truth. Why else would I be here?'

'You tell me.' Rafaello's thin mouth compressed as he turned back to the road.

Jaime felt more than a little indignant. 'I didn't ask for this invitation,' she said tautly.

Rafaello's brown-fingered hands tightened on the wheel. 'Then why have you come here? I would have thought an invitation to the Castello di Vaggio was the last thing you might accept.'

'And you'd be right.' Jaime was stung into retaliation. 'I knew you wouldn't approve.'

'Would you expect me to?'

Jaime found she was breathing shallowly and took a deep gulp of air. 'I came because Nicola asked me to come,' she declared tersely. 'I had hoped she would meet me, and that any conversation between the two of *us* would be in the company of other people. I didn't know Nicola was not going to be well enough to drive so far, or that you might see this as an opportunity to re-open old hostilities!'

Rafaello cast a mocking look in her direction. 'How cold you are, Miss Forster!' he observed scornfully. 'How controlled! I can hardly conceive that I once believed you were a warm human being, a creature of flesh and blood! It was a weakness on your part, no doubt, and one which you have evidently succeeded in destroying. Forgive me for reminding you of times you would prefer to forget.'

Jaime's nostrils flared. 'Why do you persist in

calling me Miss Forster? Don't you think that's a little petty?'

'Petty?' He lifted his shoulders uncomprehendingly. 'What is petty?'

'Mean—small-minded.' Jaime's fists clenched. 'And insulting me is rather childish, isn't it?'

'Was I doing that?' Rafaello's tone had hardened nevertheless. 'I am sorry. I keep forgetting you are still a woman.'

Jaime's fingers itched to strike the arrogant expression from his face, but the *autostrada* was not the place to indulge her temper. Besides, he should not know he could get under her skin so easily, and she steeled herself to ride his abuse without exhibiting any obvious reaction.

'You are the assistant to the company director now, are you not?' he remarked, a few minutes later, and she forced herself to look at him.

'Is there anything wrong with that?'

'No.' He paused. 'You have flown high and wide since those early days. The humble typist becomes the sophisticated business executive. Tell me, have you found your job as satisfying as you thought it would be?'

'Completely,' replied Jaime crisply, concentrating on the curve of the road ahead, though she was aware of Rafaello's eyes upon her.

'In all ways?' he persisted, the tenor of his voice deepening as he spoke, and Jaime's resentment grew at the deliberate way he was attempting to disrupt her self-possession.

'In all ways,' she assured him, meeting his scornful gaze. 'There's more to life than meekly accommodating a man's sexual instincts, if that's what you mean. A woman should learn to use her head as well as her body.'

'As you have?' snapped Rafaello harshly, and Jaime nodded.

'Why not?'

His jaw hardened. 'I take it you don't regret— anything.'

'No. Why should I?' She paused. 'Do you?'

Rafaello's thick lashes narrowed his eyes as he turned back again to the road. 'What have I to regret?' he stated bleakly. 'I never knew you.'

There was silence for a time after that, while Jaime endeavoured to recover her composure. Much to her dismay, Rafaello's last words had scraped a nerve, and she found to her chagrin that her hands were shaking and her knees felt disturbingly weak. She had thought that nothing he could say would disconcert her, but she had been wrong. His final denunciation had left her feeling raw and vulnerable, and she wished with all her heart that Nicola had not abandoned her to her husband's less than tender mercies.

About thirty kilometres east of Pisa, Rafaello drove off the *autostrada* on to the narrower country roads that led up into the Tuscan hills. All about them now was the rolling Italian countryside, with its patchwork of green fields interspersed with silvery-green olive groves and acres of vines. Thickly-wooded hills overlooked valleys where the wheat was already turning golden in the heat, and as the late afternoon sunlight shimmered hazily over church spires and cast shadows across the glistening curve of the river, Jaime forgot her misgivings in the sheer delight of being there.

'It's beautiful!' she breathed, as the Maserati crested a rise and the whole panorama of a milk-and-honey valley was spread out below them. 'I didn't know—I never dreamed it would be like this!'

'Would it have made any difference?' asked Rafaello flatly, and then, as if prepared to meet her halfway, he added: 'They say nature outdid herself in Tuscany. I love it, of course. It is my home, my land, my heritage! I could never give it up.'

Jaime shook her head. 'I can understand that.' She lifted her eyes. 'Is that a monastery up there?'

Rafaello followed her gaze. Clinging to the hillside several hundred feet above them, the white walls of an ancient building stood out in sharp relief, and his lips curved in a wry smile. It was the first time she had seen anything close to humour soften his stern features since they had met at the airport, and the difference it made was amazing. Gone were the grim lines that bracketed his mouth; gone, too, was the frowning cleft between his dark brows; and the parting of his lips revealed the uneven attractiveness of strong white teeth.

'It was,' he conceded, turning his attention to the road again, as they descended a sharp series of bends into the little town of Santo Giustino. 'It is an hotel now; small and spartan, it is true, but capable of accommodating perhaps a dozen people.'

'I'd like to stay there,' said Jaime, looking back over her shoulder. 'The view must be magnificent.'

'I imagine it must be.' Rafaello negotiated the narrow entry to the main square of the town. He glanced at his watch. 'You must be thirsty. We will stop here for a drink before continuing our journey.'

Jaime was surprised. 'Is it much further?' she asked, as he pulled the Maserati off the road and into a narrow parking space.

'Maybe forty kilometres,' answered Rafaello carelessly, pushing open his door. 'Come, we will have a drink at the café.'

Jaime got out of the car with some reluctance. Forty kilometres was not far – a matter of some twenty-five miles. Hardly a great distance. Wouldn't it have been simpler to drive straight to the Castello? After what Rafaello had said, she couldn't believe he had any desire to prolong this journey.

But it was too late now for misgivings. Rafaello was locking the car doors, and as her jacket was locked inside, Jaime had no choice but to accompany him as she was. Not that what she was wearing was in any way out of place in a town that catered frequently for tourists. But she was aware of Rafaello's eyes upon her, and that was what troubled her most.

Santo Giustino was a pretty little town, made the more so by the strings of coloured bunting strung out across the narrow streets. It was very old, with shops and houses set close together, and backed by a beautiful little cathedral, also decorated with flowers.

'It is carnival time,' explained Rafaello, as they crossed the square to where several tables had been set outside the doors of a small restaurant. 'Tomorrow there will be a procession of floats, and a *festa* with fireworks, celebrating the feast of Santo Gennaro.' He grimaced ruefully. 'In fact, the feast of Santo Gennaro should take place in January, but who can enjoy a *festa* when there is snow on the hills and a cold wind blows down from the Alps?'

Jaime smiled at him. She couldn't help herself, and for a moment Rafaello shared her amusement. His lean, attractive features mirrored her enjoyment, and then, as if a barrier had dropped between them, he turned away, gesturing to her to take a seat while he went to find the proprietor.

They drank Campari and soda, sitting on opposite sides of the small table, with its blue and white chequered cloth. As the shadows lengthened, more people emerged to stroll in and out of the shops that edged the square, or joined them at the tables, to talk and share a bottle of wine. It was all very peaceful and civilised, but Jaime felt anything but calm. She was only conscious of Rafaello's brooding preoccupation, and the knowledge that despite his concern for her welfare, he could not relax in her presence.

'Could we—could we spend a moment in the cathedral?' she ventured, when both their glasses were empty and it was obvious he was about to suggest going back to the car. 'I adore old churches, and this one is very old, isn't it? La Cattedrale de Santo Giustino—I read it on that notice over there,' she added apologetically. 'Please. I'd like to see inside.'

Rafaello glanced at his watch once again and got to his feet. 'If you wish,' he declared, without expression, and taking a deep breath, Jaime accompanied him round the square and up the four shallow stone steps that led into the candlelit interior of the small cathedral.

It was not like any cathedral Jaime had seen before. Its size precluded any impressive displays of architecture, but its atmosphere was instilled with the generations of believers who had worshipped here.

She noticed Rafaello crossed himself as they entered the nave, dipping his hand into the holy water and making a silent obeisance. Not having been brought up in any particular belief herself, Jaime nonetheless envied him his faith, and she bowed her head respectfully as she wandered up the aisle.

The altar was lit by two tall candelabra, and to one side there was a statue of the Virgin and child, with several unlit candles waiting to be used. 'To light a candle for someone you love is an act of faith,' remarked Rafaello behind her, stretching past her to put several coins in the collection box. 'But faith is not something you know much about, is it, Jaime?' he added, as she turned quickly to look at him.

He was close, too close, in the shadowy confines of the beautiful little church. The neck of his cream shirt was open, exposing the strong column of his throat, and from the opening she could smell the warm scent of his body. It was a disturbing scent, clean and essentially male, and her breath caught in her throat. 'The last time I saw you was in a cathedral, did you know that?' she asked huskily, her voice revealing a little of the strain she was under, and Rafaello looked at her from between narrowed lids.

'You came to the church?' he demanded. And then, with rough passion: 'Why?'

Jaime forced a lighter tone. 'I—was invited, remember?'

'You said you would not come.'

'I changed my mind.' She shrugged her slim shoulders. 'A woman's prerogative.'

Rafaello's breathing was ragged. 'You would have made a beautiful bride,' he said unsteadily. 'So tall—

so slender—so fair.' In the flickering light from the candles, his dark face was taut with emotion, and because Jaime was wearing high-heeled sandals, their eyes were almost on a level. Compulsively, it seemed, he lifted his hand to slide its length against the curve of her cheek, and in the incense-laden atmosphere, Jaime's senses spun away . . .

'*A che ora si parte, padre?*'

The youthful voice of a boy, dressed in the robes of a novice and speaking to an elderly man attired in a priest's hassock, broke the spell. One moment, Rafaello's hand was against her cheek, his thumb brushing her lips, his cool fingers incredibly sensuous against her heated skin, his dark eyes moving over her face with something akin to hunger—and the next, he had turned from her and was striding down the nave and out of the cathedral, his long legs extending the distance between them, as if by doing so he could put her out of his life.

Jaime followed more slowly. Pausing for a moment to light one of the candles and secure it in place, she nodded diffidently to the elderly priest, who had watched Rafaello's departure with evident perplexity. '*Vada con Dio, signorina,*' he murmured, making the sign of the cross, and Jaime bowed her head respectfully as she emerged from the cathedral into the slanting sunlight of the evening.

CHAPTER THREE

JAIME'S room overlooked the curve of the valley and the lower, wooded slopes of the mountains that gave it protection. It did not have the most impressive view of any of the rooms in the Castello, nor was it the largest apartment in the castle, but Jaime had been so relieved to see it, she had cared little for its size or situation.

Awakening the next morning in a bed whose proportions were totally out of place in such modest surroundings, Jaime lay for several minutes wishing she did not have to get up. The prospect of the day ahead filled her with apprehension, and she knew, without a shadow of a doubt, that she should not have given in to Nicola's pleading.

The night before, they had arrived at the Castello when the drifting shadows of evening were casting a misty insubstantiality over the surrounding country-side. The latter part of the journey had been by far the most arduous, not only because of Rafaello's brooding silence, but also because the last few miles had been a twisting turning climb through picture-book scenery that nevertheless was harrowing on the nerves. Perhaps if Rafaello had driven less aggressively, more consideringly, Jaime would not have felt as if her head was spinning by the time they reached the little town of Vaggio su Ravino, but as it was, nausea was her most obvious reaction when she first saw Rafaello's home.

The Castello di Vaggio was about half a mile from the town, at the head of a winding road that Jaime guessed would be treacherous in winter. And it was a castle, she discovered in amazement, clinging to the mountains in much the same way as the monastery she had admired earlier. Somehow, she had imagined that the name *castello* was just the courtesy title for a rather large villa, and to discover that Rafaello's ancestors had built the castle hundreds of years before had come as quite a shock. He had never boasted of his antecedents. He had never even mentioned that the di Vaggio family had lived in this part of Italy for more than eight hundred years. But Nicola had told her, spilling the castle's history carelessly as she showed Jaime to her room, answering her questions without enthusiasm, and obviously finding the subject tiresome when she wanted to talk about herself.

Nicola had been waiting for them the night before. When the sleek Maserati swept beneath the stone gateway that gave access to the courtyard, she had emerged from the castle, her flowing velvet caftan giving an impression of an earlier age.

Rafaello, who had not spoken since they left Santo Giustino, paused to give Jaime a tight look before thrusting his door open. 'My wife appears to have recovered,' he remarked, rescuing her jacket from the back of the car and tossing it into her lap. 'You will find she often has these attacks. But do not worry, she is not as fragile as she looks.'

'But——'

Jaime started to speak, but Rafaello was not listening to her. He had already thrust his legs out of the car, and as he got to his feet, Nicola reached them.

'You're late,' she pouted, looking up at her husband with resentful eyes. 'I've been waiting for ages. Was Jaime's plane late?'

'So far as I know, it was on time,' replied Rafaello, flexing his weary shoulder muscles. 'We came as quickly as we could. However, you will appreciate that I do not have the ability to rid our roads of other traffic!'

'Don't be cross.' Nicola's lips tilted. 'What must Jaime think of us?' She reached up to press her lips against his taut cheek, her eyes darting sideways as the other girl got out of the car. '*Caro*,' she murmured huskily, her fingers seeking the parted vee of his shirt, and then stepped back with a provoking smile as Rafaello dashed her hands away. Without looking at his wife again, he strode away across the courtyard, disappearing through the doorway that Nicola previously had used.

Jaime, not knowing what to make of what she had seen, made an effort to behave naturally. Going round to the back of the car, she fumbled awkwardly for the catch of the boot, but Nicola, after following her husband's retreating figure with her eyes, seemed to remember her manners, and came eagerly to embrace her.

'I'm sorry,' she said, the look of provocation quite gone now, and replaced by a distinctly tearful expression. 'Oh, Jaime,' she hugged her very close, 'you don't know how good it is to see you again! You must forgive me if I seem thoughtless, but Raf can be so cruel at times.'

'That's all right. It's good to see you, too, Nicola.' Jaime drew away determinedly, immediately aware of how gauche Nicola always made her feel. She had changed little, hardly at all, in fact, and her diminutive height of a little over five feet had always made Jaime feel like an Amazon. A cap of glossy dark hair framed a face that might have modelled a Botticelli angel, and in those early days Jaime had often marvelled that Rafaello had not chosen Nicola from the beginning. She was so much more to his taste, after all, not least because Nicola had had no ambitions beyond making a good marriage, and she had done her best to catch his attention before Jaime came on the scene.

'Leave your luggage,' exclaimed Nicola impatiently now. 'Giulio will attend to it. You must be starving. We'll go and have dinner, and then I'll show you your room.'

After the journey Jaime had just had, she would have preferred to go straight to her room. A shower and a change of clothes would have been very welcome, but as Nicola's guest, she felt obliged to fall in with her wishes. But afterwards . . .

It was deliciously cool inside the thick walls of the castle. Outside, the evening was quite humid, but inside an air-conditioning system that required no electricity kept the atmosphere fresh.

'I thought it would be incredibly cold in winter,' confessed Nicola, leading the way across a marble-tiled hall, with suits of armour set beneath fading tapestries, 'but it's not. As a matter of fact, it can be quite cosy; although I must admit I prefer the apartment in Rome.'

'The apartment?' echoed Jaime, gazing about her with fascinated eyes. An inlaid marble staircase swept above them in a veined pinkish semi-circle, and a vaulted ceiling arched above a mural gallery.

'Of course.' Nicola led the way into an oblong-shaped dining room, where a rectangular table was set with three places. 'Didn't you know Raf had an apartment in Rome? He has a house in Florence, too, and a *palazzo* in Venice. He's a rich man, Jaime. Surely you knew that.'

'I knew.' Jaime schooled her features not to show any expression but one of polite interest. 'You live here, though.'

'Most of the time—unfortunately,' declared Nicola, with a tightening of her lips. 'Raf insists on being near his blasted vines. All the other *vigneti* leave the growing of the grapes to their estate *capos*. But not Raf!'

She pulled impatiently at a velvet cord, hanging beside a screened fireplace, and presently a woman, dressed all in black, appeared. 'We will eat now, Maria,' Nicola declared, as Jaime moved to look out of the long windows. 'Will you tell the *signore* we are waiting?'

'*Credo che sia partito, signora,*' murmured the woman apologetically, and Jaime, turning from the window, saw the look of anger that crossed Nicola's face.

'Speak English, can't you?' she exclaimed, her fists clenching tightly at her sides. 'Where is he? Where has he gone? He knew we were about to have dinner.'

'*Ill conte*—the *signore*—he has gone to the—to the *vigneti, signora,*' stammered Maria, spreading her hands. '*Mi spiace——*'

'Oh, bring in the food!' ordered Nicola shortly, lifting the carafe the woman had left on the table, and pouring herself a glass of red wine. '*Pronto,* Maria!'

'*Si, signora.*'

Maria withdrew and Nicola raised the glass to her lips. 'I suppose you think I was hard on her,' she remarked, observing Jaime's doubtful expression. She swallowed a mouthful of the wine. 'The woman's a fool! She should have told me immediately where Raf had gone.'

'Where—has he gone?' asked Jaime, not sure she had interpreted Maria's words correctly, and Nicola waved the hand holding the glass in a gesture of resignation.

'He's gone down to the winery,' she declared carelessly. 'I told you, Raf cares more about his vines than he does about—practically anything.' She pulled a heavily carved chair away from the table. 'Sit down, can't you? We don't stand on ceremony here.'

The meal that followed was deliciously flavoured and expertly presented. Slices of cured ham were offered with cubes of iced melon; there was a fragrant vegetable soup, and eggs served with pasta, and *pizza*, piled high with tomatoes and cheese and anchovies. There was crisp salad, and fresh fruit, and cheeses, both sweet and savoury, and wine of various vintages, looking magnificent in tall, long-stemmed glasses.

But Jaime had no stomach to appreciate any of it. She didn't like the undercurrents here. She didn't care for the way Nicola treated the servants, or understand her mood that alternated between a touching gentleness and a brittle impatience. One moment she seemed subdued and appealing, arousing Jaime's compassion when she spoke of the loneliness she suffered here, miles from her friends and family. She scarcely understood the language, she said, and although most of the servants could speak English, they lapsed into their own tongue whenever she came near.

Yet, to counter this impression of devoted womanhood, was Nicola's attitude when Jaime suggested she should talk to Rafaello, explain the situation and try to make him see the problems she was experiencing. Then Nicola became quite agitated, dismissing Jaime's words with an hysterical outburst, declaring that Rafaello wouldn't talk to her, that he didn't understand her, and that there were times when she wished she was dead.

Lying in bed now, Jaime felt the faintest trace of a headache stirring just behind her temples. It was probably the amount of wine she had drunk the night before, she decided, refusing to admit the possibility that her unease about her visit here could be responsible. After all, Nicola was not in any immediate danger. She was disturbed, certainly, but given time they might be able to work something out. It was not her problem. She had come here at Nicola's request and she would leave as soon as she had convinced her that this was something she had to handle herself. She was not a psychiatrist, she was not even a marriage guidance counsellor, and Nicola had to be made to see that Rafaello was the obvious person to turn to.

Sliding out of bed, Jaime padded barefoot across the carpeted floor and peered weakly through the blinds. It was another sunlit morning, and when she pushed the window open she could smell the fragrance of newly-cut grass. It was still early, barely eight o'clock, but the sound of horse's hooves from the yard below drew her attention from the shining curve of the river and its banks starred with daisies. Rafaello and another man were leading two horses out of the courtyard and on to the hillside beyond, and Jaime drew back out of sight, afraid that he might think she was spying on him.

He had not returned when Nicola showed her to her room the night before, and although the other girl would have lingered, Jaime begged to be excused. She was confused and she was tired, and she wanted desperately to be alone to think about everything that had happened. Nicola had eventually left her with the somewhat disturbing injunction that they would have plenty of time to talk today.

Yet now here was Rafaello, the cause of her friend's unhappiness, if Nicola was to be believed, embarking on an early morning outing with every sign of pleasured anticipation at the prospect. This morning, too, he looked more relaxed than he had done last evening. Gone were the expensive jacket and well-cut trousers he had worn the day before. In their place, tight-fitting jeans clung to his thighs, pushed into knee-length leather boots; and instead of the fine silk shirt Jaime remembered, a rough cotton jerkin was stretched across his chest. It exposed the upper part of his chest, exposed the brown skin, the muscles taut beneath, and Jaime knew a sudden dizziness at the remembrance of how smooth his skin had felt against hers. 'Skin on skin,' he had said, pulling her down on top of him in his suite at the hotel in London, and the afternoon had slid away as so many afternoons had done . . .

Jaime turned back from the window abruptly, pushing back the tumbled weight of her hair with an unsteady hand. This would not do, she told herself fiercely. She had not come here to re-live old memories. She had come because Nicola had begged her to do so, and the sooner she set about achieving her objective the better.

Ignoring the sounds from beyond the windows, she pushed her feet into fluffy mules and went into the bathroom. Like her room, which had only the minimum of furnishings, the bathroom, too, was of spartan design. A huge white bath with clawed feet, a matching basin, and a lavatory set up on a kind of dais completed its fitments, along with a noisy water-tank, that protested every time she turned on the taps. She had taken a bath the night before, so now she contented herself with a rather lukewarm wash before returning to the bedroom.

Giulio, whoever that might be, had delivered her suitcase the night before, and it had been there waiting for her when Nicola showed her to her apartments. As she rummaged through the case now, grateful that modern clothes required little attention, Jaime wondered if she would be able to find her way downstairs again. Nicola had made no apology for the distance she had had to walk, but judging by her situation in relation to the courtyard below, she should be able to find her way down.

Deciding to follow Rafaello's example, Jaime put on a pair of white denim slacks and a lime-green cotton shirt, with elbow-length sleeves that ended in a cuff. Ignoring the chiding voice inside her that scorned her decision to put on flat sandals instead of her usual four-inch heels, she brushed her hair and leaving it loose, tied a narrow scarf, bandanna-fashion, around her forehead.

Within the walls of the castle, there seemed to be few sounds, or perhaps that was because she was nowhere near its other occupants, Jaime reflected ruefully, descending the winding stairway to the first floor. She seemed to have been accommodated in one of the turrets of the castle, and she refused to panic when she reached a fork in the passageway and realised she had no idea which direction to take.

A narrow window gave her her bearings, and choosing the left of the two passageways, she crossed her fingers and followed it. She was unutterably relieved when it finally emerged into the gallery at the top of the main staircase, and trailing her fingers along the cool marble balustrade, she descended to the hall below.

She could hear someone singing now, in one of the apartments off to her right, and as she reached the bottom of the stairs, a girl appeared, carrying an armful of fresh linen.

'*Buon giorno, signorina.*'

The girl addressed her politely, and would have passed her to go up the stairs, but Jaime put her hand out to detain her. 'Er—*buon giorno*,' she echoed, hoping the girl would not imagine she was familiar with her language. 'I wonder—am I too early for breakfast?'

'Breakfast, *signorina*?' The girl's dark brows ascended. 'Ah—no, *signorina*. *La signora*, she is not having breakfast.'

'Oh?' Jaime looked as perplexed as she felt, and she turned with some relief, when another voice interrupted them. 'She means the *signora* does not eat breakfast, *signorina*,' the young man who had appeared from behind the stairs said easily. 'Signora di Vaggio has forgotten the English habit of bacon and eggs.'

'Oh, no!' Jaime uttered a relieved laugh. 'I don't eat bacon and eggs either.' She was very conscious of his dark eyes appraising her as she spoke, and she had to acknowledge he was a handsome creature. 'I just wondered if I could get some coffee, that's all. If it's no trouble.'

'It's no trouble,' he assured her, returning her smile with admiring eyes. '*Se ne vada*, Lucia. *Lasci fare a me.*'

'*Si, signore. Signorina.*'

The girl bobbed and hurried on up the stairs, but Jaime was aware that she glanced back from time to time. Evidently, whoever he was, her companion had some authority over the servants, but the girl's attitude towards him had not been one of diffidence.

As if reading her thoughts, the man spoke again: 'Allow me to introduce myself,' he said. 'My name is Lorenzo Costa. I am the—chauffeur—to the Conte.'

His chauffeur! Jaime's tongue came to circle her lips in a thoughtful motion. Did that account for his familiarity; for the feeling she had that Lorenzo Costa had a high opinion of his talents?

'Well, I'm very grateful to you, Signor Costa,' she murmured, with a bow of her head. 'I'm afraid my Italian is limited to phrases like: *sono inglese*, and *non capisco*, and *come stá!*'

'Your accent is very good,' he applauded her smilingly. 'What a pity you do not speak our language fluently. There are other phrases I would like to hear from your lips.'

Jaime laughed. She couldn't help herself. Probably,

it wouldn't be considered very proper to fraternise with the staff, but it was such a relief to speak to someone who presented no threat to her hard-won independence.

'Have you worked here long, Signor Costa?' she asked, noticing how white his shirt was against his dark skin. He was wearing black trousers and a black wasitcoat, and she could imagine that in his uniform he would offer quite a challenge to the female members of the staff.

'The Conte employed me two years ago, *signorina*,' he responded, lifting his broad shoulders. Though he was not so tall as Rafaello, he was more sturdily built, and the muscles in his arms rippled as he moved. 'And my name is Lorenzo,' he added dryly.

'Lorenzo.' Jaime repeated his name. 'I see.' She smiled. 'Well, Lorenzo, do you think it would be possible for me to have a cup of coffee?'

'*Ma certo, signorina*,' he declared, giving her a mocking little bow, and pointing her towards the dining room, he disappeared in the direction of the kitchen.

To her surprise, he brought her breakfast himself, appearing perhaps ten minutes later with a tray containing a pot of coffee, with cream and sugar, a dish of croissants, a jar of strawberry conserve, and curls of yellow butter.

Jaime, who had been leaning on the stone window ledge, looking down over the rooftops of Vaggio su Ravino several hundred feet below, turned in surprise at his entrance. 'Maria is busy,' he said carelessly, setting the tray down on the polished table. '*Vene*. The croissants have just come out of the oven.'

Jaime shook her head. 'Thank you.'

'*Mio piacere*,' he assured her easily, and at her look of incomprehension, he added: 'My pleasure.'

Jaime took her seat at the table and looked up at him helplessly. 'I wish you would join me.'

'Regrettably, that is not possible,' he averred, with a smile. 'But, after you have eaten, I would be happy to show you a little more of the castle, if you wish.'

Jaime hesitated. 'Signora di Vaggio——'

'Signora di Vaggio does not usually rise much before noon, *signorina*,' Lorenzo assured her confidently. 'I will return in fifteen minutes. You can let me know your decision then.'

The coffee was strong, and Jaime took it black with two spoonfuls of sugar. The croissants were, as Lorenzo had said, hot from the oven, and although she had not thought she was hungry, Jaime found the creamy yellow butter and real strawberries irresistible. By the time Lorenzo returned, she had eaten three of them, and his smile was knowing as she wiped her mouth on the napkin.

'You are ready?' he asked, as she pushed back her chair and Jaime nodded.

'If you're sure that Nico—I mean, Signora di Vaggio is not an early riser.'

'You will find out,' remarked Lorenzo, stepping back to allow her to precede him out the door. 'Come, this way. I will show you the gardens.'

They went out the door through which Jaime had entered the night before. In daylight, with the sun glinting on its rough stonework and sparkling like diamonds on its jewelled panes, the castle had an entirely different aspect from the one she had

imagined the night before. Or perhaps it was that the
atmosphere today was not tainted by the row that had
erupted between Rafaello and his wife, and Jaime
could look about her with interest and not apprehension.

'The inside of the Castello was not much more than
a ruin when *il conte*'s father inherited it,' observed
Lorenzo, as Jaime looked up at its solid walls. 'It was
many years since anyone had lived here, and what with
the war . . .' He shrugged. 'The old *conte* spent a small
fortune restoring it to a family home again. The
present *conte* was born here, and so, too, was his son.'

'His son!' Jaime turned to Lorenzo with evident
consternation. 'I mean—I didn't know Raf—the
count—had a son.'

'He does not.' Lorenzo shrugged his broad
shoulders. 'The child was born too soon. It was
already dead, when the *dottore* took it from its
mother.'

Jaime looked down at the gravelled sweep of the
courtyard. She had not known. She had not guessed.
But then why should she? Until Nicola rang, she had
known nothing of her life in Italy.

'It was very sad,' said Lorenzo, although he didn't
sound particularly concerned. 'See, through this
archway are the stables. Do you ride, *signorina*?'

Jaime gathered herself with difficulty. 'What? Oh—
yes, a little. We were taught to ride at school, but it's
years——'

'One does not forget, I think.' Lorenzo made an
eloquent gesture. 'You would make a good horse-
woman. So straight the back, so long the legs.' He
gave her an admiring look. 'Unlike the *signora*. She does

not ride. She is too small to control a horse.'

Jaime refused to respond to his knowing glance. 'You're an expert, I suppose,' she remarked drily, putting his earlier comments aside, and Lorenzo grinned.

'Of horses? An expert, no. Regrettably. *Il conte* cares a great deal for his horses. Come, I will show you our latest addition.'

Jaime wished he had not brought up Rafaello's name again, but she followed him obediently into the musky atmosphere of the stables, and made suitable noises when he showed her to a stall where a mare and her foal were tethered.

'This is Sylvana, and the little one is called Mazolino,' said Lorenzo, resting his arms on the rail. 'See how strong the little one is. Primato—*il conte*'s *stallone*—he—how would you say?—fathered him.'

'Sired,' corrected Jaime, unable to resist touching the colt's shiny coat, and Lorenzo nodded.

'*Si*, he sired the little one. He has a strong seed.'

'Yes, well——' Jaime turned away to walk out of the stables, pausing only briefly to pat the nose of another horse leaning over the gate of its stall. 'You were going to show me the gardens.'

'I have embarrassed you?'

Lorenzo joined her outside as she was blinking to adjust her eyes to the light, and Jaime gave him a wry look. 'No, you haven't embarrassed me,' she replied flatly. Then, countering: 'Were you trying to?'

Lorenzo grinned. 'Perhaps. You intrigue me, *signorina*. I know you are a friend of the *signora*'s, yet you seem to know *il conte* very well. That is unusual, you must admit.'

Jaime kept her expression neutral. 'Why? I have known Nicola for years. Long before she married your employer.'

Lorenzo inclined his head. 'If you say so, *signorina*.'

'I do.'

Jaime had difficulty in maintaining her indifference. There was something disturbingly familiar about Lorenzo's attitude, and while she was not afraid that she might not be able to handle him, she couldn't help wondering if Rafaello was aware of his arrogance.

The stables had evidently once been quite extensive, but now they were partly converted for garage use. Through one of the open doorways, Jaime glimpsed the gleaming lines of a vintage Alfa-Romeo, but rather than encourage Lorenzo to think she wanted to be alone with him, she made no comment.

Beyond the stables, an arched doorway set in the wall gave on to the terraced gardens. The hillside had been cut away to form flower and vegetable gardens, and roses and verbena scented the air with their perfume. There were alpine plants adorning a rockery, a low stone wall covered with trailing ferns, and a sloping expanse of lawn, that someone kept manicurely smooth. A stand of cypress formed a natural windbreak, and a shallow flight of steps led down to a path that disappeared into the trees.

'You can see Monteravino from here,' declared Lorenzo, following her down the steps and pausing to point past her shoulder. 'That way,' he said, his breath fanning her cheek, and as she turned to look at him, she saw Nicola watching them from the arched doorway.

She was immediately conscious of how her closeness

to Lorenzo might appear to Nicola, and taking a step backward, she said: 'I thought you said Signora di Vaggio didn't get up in the mornings.'

Lorenzo glanced back over his shoulder. 'She does not—usually,' he assured her, in a low tone.

Jaime shook her head, and leaving him standing there, she walked swiftly up the steps and along the flagged path to where Nicola was waiting. 'Good morning,' she said, aware that the other girl's dress of ice-blue silk and perfect make-up must contrast sharply with her own casual appearance. 'I thought you were not an early riser. You don't mind that Lorenzo's been showing me around?'

Nicola's expression was hard to read, but her annoyance was evident in the way she spoke. 'You could have waited for me, Jaime,' she declared, her eyes moving past her to Lorenzo, picking his way more slowly towards them. 'Or was the temptation too great, I wonder?' Her lips snapped shut, and then: 'You certainly don't waste any time, do you?'

Jaime was amazed, and indignant. 'I beg your pardon——' she began, and then broke off abruptly as Lorenzo reached them and halted right behind her.

'*Buon giorno, signora!*' he greeted Nicola, with a curious mixture of deference and mockery. '*Che sorpresa!*'

Nicola's eyes flashed angrily. 'Where have you been?'

'Where have I been?' Lorenzo quirked one dark eyebrow. 'Why, I have been entertaining your so-beautiful friend, *signora*. I knew you would wish me to do so. You would not wish her to be alone.'

Nicola's teeth clenched. '*Porco!*' she said, and then,

realising that Jaime was watching this exchange with something like astonishment, she quickly changed back to English.

'Come, Jaime,' she said, turning back into the courtyard. 'Maria has made some fresh lemonade. Let's go up to my room.' She cast a scornful look in Lorenzo's direction. 'We can talk privately there.'

With a helpless backward glance at the chauffeur, Jaime followed Nicola along the path, past the stables, across the courtyard and into the house. Lorenzo followed them as far as the garages, and then raised his hand in silent farewell. Jaime, pausing in the doorway to the castle, glimpsed his mocking salute, and wondered, with a feeling of unease, why she had the distinct impression that Nicola was jealous . . .

CHAPTER FOUR

In all honesty, Jaime had no desire to visit the rooms Nicola shared with Rafaello, but she could hardly refuse without arousing suspicion. Besides, she told herself severely, as she accompanied Nicola up the sweeping staircase, it should make no difference to her what their sleeping arrangements might be, and it was not for Rafaello's sake she had agreed to make this journey.

The principal apartments of the castle were close to the head of the stairs. Jaime followed Nicola into a luxurious gold and blue sitting room, with a sumptuous archway giving access to an equally luxurious bedroom. The carpets were soft and deeply piled, the furnishings were all satin and damask, and the enormous bed that occupied a central position would easily have accommodated half a dozen.

'Sit down,' said Nicola, waving towards a pair of striped Regency armchairs, but Jaime had moved to look out the window, and perched instead on the padded window-seat.

Nicola looked as though she might like to object, but the appearance with a tray of one of the maids diverted her. 'Put it there,' she ordered, indicating a small table, and catching Jaime's eye added: *'Grazie!'* with a certain amount of impatience.

When the door was closed again, Nicola lifted the jug of iced lemonade and offered it to the other girl.

'Just a little,' said Jaime, wishing she was still outside on such a lovely morning, and Nicola poured two glasses before coming to stand beside her.

'Thank you.' Jaime took the glass Nicola offered her and indicated the padded bench beside her. 'Why don't you sit down, too? It's a wonderful view.'

'You think so?' Nicola was offhand, retreating to take one of the striped armchairs and crossing her legs rather irritably. 'I'm afraid this place gets on my nerves.'

'But why?' Jaime was surprised. 'It's not as if it's primitive in any way.'

'Isn't it?' Nicola was edgy. 'Have you any idea of the thickness of these walls?'

Jaime sighed. 'Is that important?'

'It is to me.' Nicola swallowed her lemonade with one gulp, and then getting to her feet disappeared through the archway into the bedroom. When she returned, she was carrying a small silver flask, and as Jaime watched, she poured a little of the pale-coloured liquid it contained into her glass. 'Don't look like that!' she exclaimed. 'It's only brandy. Sometimes I think I'd go mad if Lorenzo didn't get this for me.'

Lorenzo! Jaime looked down into her glass. Was that why he had adopted that air of patronage in Nicola's presence?

'Anyway,' Nicola resumed her seat, and took a generous mouthful of the spirit, 'you didn't come here to discuss my drinking habits, did you? I'm not an alcoholic, or anything ghastly like that. There are just times . . .'

She let the sentence trail away, and Jaime shook her head. 'It's still barely eleven o'clock in the morning,

Nicola,' she said. 'Do you think it's wise to risk your health——'

'My health!' Nicola interrupted her shrilly. 'What does my health have to do with anything? I'm healthy enough. It's Raf! He's the one you should blame. It's his fault that I'm in this state.'

'Calm down!' Jaime was disturbed. 'I'm not criticising you, Nicola. I simply don't understand what all this is about.'

Nicola hunched her shoulders. 'How could you? You haven't cared if I was dead or alive for the past five years!'

'That's not true.' Jaime spread her free hand. 'Nicola, you know as well as I do that Raf—well, it was easier for all of us to drift apart. We had nothing in common, after all, and you seemed contented enough.'

Nicola sniffed. 'I was—then.'

'So——' Jaime was loath to ask it, 'what went wrong?'

'Nothing. Everything.' Nicola spoke dramatically. 'Oh, Jaime, you have no idea . . .'

'Would it make it any easier for you if I told you that Lorenzo told me about the baby?'

'He did?' Nicola licked her lips. 'What did he tell you?'

Jaime bent her head. 'Just—that the baby had died.'

'It didn't die.' Nicola's face contorted. 'It was dead. It was dead long before they took it from me.'

'I know.' Jaime didn't know what to say to her. 'But——' her own stomach constricted at the thought, 'you'll have other children.'

'I won't.' Nicola finished the brandy in her glass

and got restlessly to her feet. 'Raf won't have any more. He blames me for losing the baby, and he refuses to consider me having another!'

'No!' Jaime looked up at her with horrified eyes. 'No, you must be mistaken.'

'I'm not.' Nicola's eyes filled with tears. 'That's what he told me.' She shook her head. 'You know how much I wanted a baby. Do you remember when we were at school and you used to talk about having a career? All I ever wanted to do was get married and have children.'

Jaime put down her glass. 'But have you talked to Raf about this?' she asked carefully, as Nicola groped for a tissue. 'I mean, surely you can't mean he's punishing you for what happened. These things happen all the time. They can happen to anyone.'

'Do you think I don't know that?' Nicola blew her nose tearfully. 'Now do you begin to understand why I'm so unhappy here? Now do you see why I had to talk to you?'

Jaime caught her lower lip between her teeth. 'Have you mentioned this to anyone else?'

'Who?'

'Well . . . your doctor.'

'Dottore Sferza?' Nicola's lips twisted. 'He's Raf's doctor, not mine.'

'But in Rome—surely there's a doctor in Rome you could consult?'

Nicola shook her head. 'What could I say? That my husband blames me for our dead child? That he refuses to consider another pregnancy?' She choked on the words. 'Could you tell a stranger that?'

Jaime lifted her shoulders helplessly. 'But I

don't see what else you can do.'

'Don't you?' Nicola wiped her nose on the tissue and approached the other girl diffidently. Perching on the edge of the window seat, she reached for one of Jaime's hands, and although Jaime did not welcome this display of emotion, she could not draw her hand away. 'Why do you think I've brought you here, Jaime?' Nicola asked, her blue eyes wide and appealing. 'There is no one else. I couldn't tell Mummy—she'd die of shame. And Daddy—well, Daddy would bluster a lot, but he'd never go against Raf in anything. He respects him too much——'

'Wait a minute!' Jaime interrupted her there, withdrawing her hand firmly and linking her fingers tightly together in her lap. 'I don't think I understand what you're saying, Nicola.'

'Of course you do.' Nicola gazed at her confidently. 'I could always talk to you.'

Jaime's mouth felt dry. 'To talk? That's why you've brought me here?'

'Of course.' But Jaime's moment of relief was short-lived. 'To talk to me—and to talk to Raf——'

'*No!*'

'—because you're the only person he's likely to listen to.'

'No!' Jaime was vehement. 'Nicola, you don't know what you're saying.'

'Jaime, Jaime,' now Nicola was the calm one, putting her point of view with subjective logic, 'don't get upset. I'm not asking so much, surely. You're the only one who knows Raf—the only one who might stand a chance of appealing to him. Can't you see? It's the least you can do.'

'The least?' Jaime was bewildered.

'Of course. We both know that if it hadn't been for you, Raf would never have married me.'

Jaime swallowed convulsively. 'I—I had nothing to do with it.'

'You know you did.' Nicola was quite dispassionate now. 'If you hadn't been so damned determined on being a career woman, you might have been in my position today.'

Jaime's colour rose. 'That has nothing to do with it.'

'Doesn't it?' Nicola was cold. 'What if I told you that on our wedding night, Raf called me *Jaime*?'

Jaime got up from the window seat, unable to sit still under Nicola's accusations. 'I—I still don't see what I can do,' she exclaimed through clenched teeth, keeping her back to Nicola, so that the other girl should not see how much her words had affected her.

'You can talk to Raf,' declared Nicola impassively. 'Appeal to him on my behalf.' She uttered a scornful laugh. 'That should prove novel, at any rate.'

Jaime swung round. 'I can't——'

'Why can't you?'

'Raf wouldn't listen to me.'

'He might. If you tell him how desperate I am.' Nicola's expression softened with one of her abrupt changes of mood. 'You don't know what it's like, Jaime. Having this—this craving inside you! I want a baby, Raf's baby. Surely you can understand that.'

Jaime drew an unsteady breath. 'If you waited a while——'

'Waited?' Nicola caught her breath. 'I've waited too long as it is. The child—*our son*—died almost three years ago. I have waited. And I can't wait any longer.'

Jaime lifted her eyes to the ceiling. She had been wise to be apprehensive, she thought emotionally. She should have known that Nicola would not have contacted her after all these years without there being some significant reason. But even if she had consulted her horoscope, or racked her brains from now until next year, she could never have guessed Nicola's motives in bringing her to the Castello di Vaggio.

'Oh, Jaime——' Nicola's sudden moan of misery attracted Jaime's unwilling attention. 'I feel sick!' she gasped, stumbling across the room towards the bedroom, but before Jaime could help her, she had collapsed in a groaning heap on the floor.

The brandy, thought Jaime impatiently, as Nicola retched violently, and her resentment turned to pity for the helpless girl at her feet. 'I'll get someone,' she exclaimed, realising she could not possibly attend to this alone, and then fell back abruptly when the door was suddenly thrust open.

Rafaello stood on the threshold, and Jaime glanced behind her uneasily, aware that Nicola would not want her husband to see her like this. 'I—could I talk to you?' she asked awkwardly, hoping he would step back into the corridor, but Raf had already comprehended the situation.

'Have you called for help?' he enquired crisply, viewing his wife's wretched condition without expression, and Jaime shook her head.

'I—I was just going for assistance,' she admitted, tucking her thumbs into the back of her jeans. 'She—I—it must have been something she ate.'

Rafaello made no response to this. He simply crossed to the bell pull Jaime had not even noticed and hauled on it heavily. Then, still without speaking, he went into the bathroom and came back seconds later with a soft apricot-coloured towel. Squatting down beside his wife, he wiped her sweating forehead, and then, as the bout of sickness subsided, he helped her to her feet.

Nicola was too giddy to care who was helping her, but Jaime's nerves tightened as Rafaello helped Nicola to the bed and began unzipping the blue silk dress which had looked so immaculate earlier. He could be so gentle, she thought, pressing her lips together, and she wished she did not feel so superfluous or so helpless.

The arrival of one of the maids gave her the opportunity she had been waiting for, and realising Nicola was in no state to know whether she was there or not, Jaime backed out of the room. She needed to get away and be on her own. She needed time to think about the things Nicola had told her. But most of all, she needed to control the crazy awareness that rapidly her emotions were overtaking her reason.

'Jaime!'

Rafaello speaking her name brought her to an unwilling standstill, and she turned at the head of the stairs to find him striding after her. In the cotton shirt and jeans he had worn to go riding, he exuded an air of raw masculinity, and away from the unpleasant atmosphere of his apartments, the heated male scent of his body was unmistakeable.

'I want to talk to you,' he said, glancing back over his shoulder. 'But not now.' He brushed a careless hand across his thigh. 'I need a shower, and a change of clothes. Meet me in the library in fifteen minutes.'

'Oh, really——' Jaime put her hand to the back of her neck, under the silky weight of her hair, 'is this necessary? I—er—I've got a headache. Couldn't it wait until later?'

'I do not think so.' Rafaello was uncompromising. 'Your headache was not so great that you could not go walking with Lorenzo in the hot sunlight, or sufficient to deter you from encouraging Nicola to drink spirits before noon.'

'Now, wait a minute——' Jaime was indignant, but Rafaello was already turning away. 'Fifteen minutes: you will wait fifteen minutes,' he declared, his dark eyes chillingly determined. 'The library, *signorina*. Any of the servants will tell you where it is.'

Jaime's lips pursed mutinously as he walked away. It was her first experience of Rafaello's arrogance, and her state of mind was such that she resolved not to obey him. She was not one of his employees; she was not a servant; and he had no right to treat her as one, just because he resented her friendship with his wife.

She decided to go to her own room. Although she would have much preferred to go outside, there was less likelihood of Rafaello finding her indoors, and she had not been lying, her head was aching quite badly now.

It was not so difficult to find her tower as she had half expected. Now that she was learning her way about the castle, it was possible to calculate her whereabouts, and she breathed a sigh of relief when she reached her own apartments.

Her bed had been made in her absence, and the room tidied and put to order. With the windows open, as she had left them, the room felt delightfully cool, and she pulled off her bandanna and collapsed on the bed, with a feeling of utter abandon. Oh, Martin, she thought wistfully, if you could see me now, you wouldn't approve at all! Somehow this warm and passionate land had infected her with its urgency, and the cool collected Jaime he had known in England had given way to a girl who was suddenly and irresponsibly governed by emotion.

Jaime had been nineteen when she first saw Rafaello di Vaggio. Unfortunately, as it turned out, it had been at the home of Nicola's parents that she had met him, and she knew Mrs Temple had never forgiven her for thwarting all her plans; albeit temporarily.

Jaime hadn't seen Nicola since they had both left Abbotsford nine months previously, Nicola to attend a finishing school in Switzerland, and Jaime to take up her position in the typing pool at Helena Holt Cosmetics. It was Christmas, and when Nicola discovered that her friend intended to spend the festive season in her bedsitter in Earl's Court, she had insisted that Jaime came to stay with her parents in Windsor.

'We're having a house party,' she said. 'One or two business colleagues of Daddy's and their wives, my aunt and uncle and my two cousins, and a rather super Italian count, who Mummy is hoping will take a fancy to me.'

Jaime had hesitated about accepting Nicola's generous invitation, but Mrs Temple herself had endorsed her daughter's sentiments. 'You can't possibly remain in that dreadful little room all over the holiday,' she had declared firmly. 'We've got plenty of room, and one more or less won't make any great difference.'

Nevertheless, Jaime had arrived at the Temples' spacious house in Windsor feeling totally out of place. Everyone else had friends or family to talk to, while apart from Nicola and her parents, she knew nobody. Until Rafaello singled her out . . .

Rolling on to her side now, Jaime traced the damask pattern of the quilt with an unsteady finger. Rafaello, she thought tautly, *Raf*—who had taken pity on her at once, and made it his business to ensure that she enjoyed herself.

And she had. Closing her eyes now, she could remember every moment of that magical weekend. From the moment Rafaello was introduced to her as a friend of Nicola's, until the night after she returned to London, when Rafaello had made love to her . . .

She supposed, in his way, he had been as much a stranger as she was. His own family was back in Italy, he said, except for his mother, who was visiting relatives in San Francisco over Christmas, but business had brought him to London, and he had been happy to accept Mr Temple's invitation.

'A bachelor uncle is of no value at Christmas,' he confessed with a smile. 'My brother and sisters all have children—*bambini*—while I can only be relied upon to produce an extra present.'

Jaime laughed. 'I expect that will change when you get married and have children of your own,' she said, and Rafaello nodded.

'*When* I do,' he conceded lazily. 'When I find someone who will take me. Until then, I am considered—how do you say it?—the black sheep of the family.'

Jaime, aware that there must be many of his fellow-countrywomen who would take him without hesitation, gave him an old-fashioned look. 'I hope you find what you're looking for,' she replied, conscious that the length of their conversation had not gone unnoticed by the Temples. 'But now, if you'll excuse me, I promised Nicola I'd help her sort out some records for dancing. It's Christmas Eve, and I believe there's to be dancing after dinner.'

Rafaello's lean fingers caught her wrist as she would have moved away. 'And afterwards?' he asked, disconcerting her by the seriousness of his gaze.

'Afterwards?' she echoed, not understanding, and he inclined his head.

'Will you come to Mass with me?' he requested, his eyes on her mouth, and Jaime gave a troubled shake of her head before pulling her hand away.

She guessed he went to the nearby Catholic church to attend the midnight service. He disappeared soon after dinner was over, and Nicola, who had been expecting to dance with him, pulled a sulky face.

'Imagine it!' she exclaimed. 'Leaving the party to go to church! Mummy's absolutely furious. She thinks it's a rejection of her hospitality.'

'I believe Italians are quite devout Catholics,' Jaime consoled her uneasily, aware that she would have enjoyed attending a religious celebration tonight of all nights. But judging by Nicola's reaction, it was lucky she had cried off. Whatever her motives, she could never have convinced the Temples that her reasons were innocent.

Christmas morning had dawned sharp and frosty. There was no snow to speak of, but the rime frost gave the illusion of a wintry scene, and in spite of her late night, Jaime was up soon after seven.

Bella, the Temples' housemaid, was already up and about, cleaning out fire grates and vacuuming the debris from the previous night's festivities. When Jaime appeared and offered to help, she at first voiced her objections, but when the girl proved to be so willing, she eventually accepted her assistance with gratitude.

So it was that when Rafaello come downstairs he found Jaime Hoovering the huge carpet in the drawing room, her hair secured beneath a shower cap Bella had provided, her creamy skin flushed with colour.

'Oh——' Jaime snatched off the cap at once, but not before Rafaello had glimpsed the delightful picture she made with moist silver tendrils curling beside her ears. 'Good morning,' she added, in some confusion, switching off the vacuum cleaner. 'I—er—if you want breakfast, you've come to the wrong place.'

'I am not hungry,' Rafaello replied huskily, tall and disturbing, in dark red corded slacks and a matching silk shirt. 'I would much prefer to watch you. Go ahead—do not let me interrupt you.'

Jaime hesitated, but she had told Bella she would do it, and she could hardly back out now. With a shrug of her slim shoulders, she switched on the Hoover and then gasped in surprise when he took it from her.

'I will do it,' he declared, brushing her objections aside. 'I may find I have missed my vocation.'

'But you can't!' exclaimed Jaime helplessly, unable to do anything to stop him. 'If Mrs Temple saw you——'

'Mrs Temple will not see me.' Rafaello swung the Hoover back and forth with superlative ease. 'There— it is done, is it not? You may put the machine away, and I will permit you to take all the credit.'

Jaime sighed, bending to wind the flex around the plastic lugs. 'I think you ought to go and see if anyone else is up,' she mumbled unhappily. 'Bella is serving breakfast in the morning room. Nicola might be there. She was looking for you last night.'

Rafaello's response was to stroke his hand across the provocative curve of her rear, and she came up with a start to find him close beside her. 'Count——' she protested, as his fingers slid along her waist to draw her nearer to him, and then her objections died beneath his lips when his mouth sought and covered hers.

She was brought close against his body, close against the taut muscles of his thighs that moulded her length against him. His lips, exploratory at first, soon demanded a deeper response, and her mouth opened helplessly under his. No man had ever kissed her as Rafaello was doing, no man had ever been permitted to hold her as Rafaello was holding her, but feeling his cool fingers sliding beneath her sweater, Jaime rapidly came to her senses.

'No!' she choked, tearing her mouth from his and putting two feet of space between them. 'I don't,' she added, rubbing the back of her hand across her bruised lips. 'That is—I think you'd better go.'

Rafaello regarded her steadily, making no move to leave her. 'What is wrong?' he asked flatly. 'There is someone else? Forgive me, but last night I thought you were free.'

'I am.' Jaime made an impatient gesture. 'That's not why I stopped you. I—just don't go in for this kind of thing.'

'What kind of thing?'

'You know.' Jaime sighed. 'I know it's Christmas, and you probably think I'm a prude, but it's not that. I just—don't want you to touch me.'

Rafaello pushed his hands into the hip pockets of his pants. 'That was not my impression.'

'No—well, perhaps you'd better confine your advances to Nicola. I don't think her mother would appreciate your spreading yourself around.'

'Nicola?' Rafaello frowned. 'What has Nicola got to do with this?'

'I think you know,' retorted Jaime unevenly. 'Now, please excuse me. I promised Bella I'd Hoover the hall, too.'

She left him then, refusing to respond to the look of blank bewilderment in his eyes. He knew perfectly well why the Temples had invited him here, she told herself fiercely. And if he thought he could play the field, then he was very much mistaken.

On Christmas afternoon, various other members of the family arrived, and Jaime was pleased to be given the opportunity to melt into the background. As the daughter of the house, Nicola attracted most attention, and although her male cousins gravitated in Jaime's direction, there were plenty of other distractions. Nevertheless, Jaime noticed Nicola seldom allowed Rafaello far from her side, and in spite of what he had said that morning, the young Italian seemed quite content to play court.

Dinner was a long and festive meal, with plenty of

good food and wine, and the pleasurable prospect of a lazy evening ahead. Only the younger members of the party joined in the dancing afterwards, and Jaime made the most of emptying ashtrays and collecting empty glasses to evade the amorous attentions of young men who had had too much to drink.

Bella went off duty at half-past nine, and Jaime was alone in the kitchen when Gavin Temple, Nicola's cousin, cornered her there. 'So this is where you've been hiding yourself,' he remarked, advancing across the wooden tiles on unsteady legs. 'Cinderella to the life, only Cinderella was never so sexy,' he added, his voice thickening ominously. 'C'mon and dance with me, Jaime. You can't stay out here all night.'

Jaime sighed, and wiped her hands on a tea-cloth. 'Go back to the party, Gavin,' she urged him quietly. 'I'll join you shortly. I just want to finish these glasses.'

'F'get the glasses,' muttered Gavin, reaching for her aggressively. 'C'mon on, stop being a spoil-sport!'

'Gavin, please——' Jaime moved round the table that stood in the middle of the floor, 'I wish you wouldn't do this. Do you want me to have to call for assistance?'

'Who from?' demanded Gavin carelessly. 'No one would hear you—they're all too busy getting drunk.' He lurched round the table towards her. 'Hey, stand still, there's a good girl.'

Jaime looked about her helplessly, searching for a weapon, but all she could see were empty bottles and she was loath to use anything so dangerous. 'Gavin——' she persisted, still glancing urgently about her, and then let out a cry of protest when his fingers grasped a handful of her hair.

'I said come here,' he grunted, pulling her towards him, and Jaime struggled furiously as his slobbering mouth descended towards hers.

'Let her go, Temple.'

The quiet command arrested Gavin in mid-flight, his eyes wobbling round unsteadily to identify the intruder. 'Clear off,' he muttered, using an ugly expletive, but when he would have resumed his previous assault, a surprisingly agile hand shot out and dragged him back.

'You clear off,' declared Rafaello grimly, 'or would you like to continue this argument outside?'

Gavin pulled himself away from the other man, brushing the shoulder of his jacket as if to remove any lingering creases Rafaello's fingers had made. 'No need to get offensive, old man,' he protested, aware of his slight height disadvantage. 'You know how it is— one minute they're all over you, and the next they're shouting rape!'

'Raf, don't!'

The words were torn from Jaime as Rafaello's fist clenched in anger, and taking advantage of the momentary distraction, Gavin stumbled towards the door. 'Better luck than I had,' he grunted, putting himself safely beyond reach, and Jaime shook her head rather hysterically as the door swung to behind him.

'Are you all right?'

Rafaello came towards her as Jaime endeavoured to recover her composure. Happily, her hair had not been too badly mussed, and the low round neckline of her fine wool dress only briefly exposed the rapid rise and fall of her breasts. With a jerky nod, she turned back to what she had been doing at the sink, and glanced at him unwillingly as he came to prop his hips against the unit beside her.

'Wh-where's Nicola?' she asked, pushing back the long sleeves of her gown so that they would not make contact with the water. 'You seemed to be having a good time.'

'You do not,' remarked Rafaello drily, nodding at the glasses. 'Do you get paid for this, or is it simply that you are avoiding me?'

'Oh, Count di Vaggio——'

'It was Raf, a few moments ago.'

'I can't call you that.'

'Why not? It is my name.' Rafaello turned and firmly drew her hands out of the water. 'Come, I want to dance with you. I promise I will not do anything you do not wish, but you cannot deny me one dance.'

Jaime sighed. 'Nicola——'

'Nicola is already dancing,' declared Rafaello steadily. 'Now, will you come?'

She couldn't resist him, even though she knew she would probably regret it in the morning. But for now, it was enough to feel him draw her into his arms, for his hands to slide about her waist, and to feel his breath fanning her temple. The music was slow, a languid refrain that had brought some of the older members of the party on to the expanse of polished wood exposed by rolling back the carpet in the dining room. In consequence, there was little room to move, and as the minutes passed, Jaime gave up trying to remain aloof. With a helpless little sigh she allowed her body to rest against him, and Rafaello unbuttoned his velvet dinner jacket to draw her inside its folds.

She felt his lips against her hair, moving along the curve of her cheek, nuzzling the sensitive hollows of her ear; but when she felt his tongue against her flesh, she flinched back from him.

'*E bene,*' he said flatly. 'It is all right. I am sorry, I will not do it again.'

When the dance was over, Jaime made her escape, uncaring what the Temples might think about her behaviour. She went upstairs, washed in the basin in her room, and undressed for bed. No doubt Gavin's loose tongue would give them a reason for why she had chosen to abandon the party, and she buried her head under the pillows, refusing to acknowledge what her sensitised flesh was evidence of.

In the morning, she was up before it was light, and putting a warm parka over narrow-legged jeans and a round-necked sweater, she left the house.

There was a park within walking distance, and she made for this, the grey dawn heralding a small army of dog-owners, all braving the winter chill to give their animals exercise. She wished the Temples had had a dog. Without any company she felt conspicuous, but happily no one seemed to take any notice.

She paused by a small lake, where a group of ducks had braved the ice to dive for food. They clucked about, ruffling their feathers, and Jaime propped herself against a tree to watch them, one booted foot raised against its bark.

'Can I join you?'

The question, spoken in a low attractive voice, sent a shiver of excitement up Jaime's spine. She turned to look at the man who had addressed her, and her pulses raced wildly at the disturbing sensuality of his mouth.

'Raf!' she breathed, her mouth dry, and he moved to stand in front of her.

'The same,' he agreed, his dark good looks accentuated by the fur-lined black jacket he was wearing. 'I heard you leave your room.'

Jaime's breathing was shallow. 'You were awake?'

'I have not been to sleep,' he amended quietly. 'Have you?'

'I—yes. Yes, of course I have,' she exclaimed, keeping her hands in her pockets.

'Then why are there these dark circles round your eyes?' enquired Rafaello softly, his fingers brushing her cheek. 'I think we are wasting time, Jaime. We should have slept together.'

'No!' Jaime turned sideways away from him. 'I mean—I wish you would stop saying these things to me. You shouldn't have come here. You shouldn't have followed me. I have to go back to London tomorrow, and Nicola won't stand for you making a fool of her.'

'To hell with Nicola!' said Rafaello, very distinctly, turning Jaime's face towards him. 'I am not interested in Nicola, I have *never* been interested in Nicola, and you make me very angry when you keep throwing her in my face!

CHAPTER FIVE

IT was very quiet in the castle room, and Jaime rolled unhappily on to her back. What was she doing? she fretted, reliving all these moments from the past. They would not help the present. They would not provide the answer to why Nicola was so unhappy. All they could do was stir uneasy memories, awaken a painful awareness that the past was not dead, only sleeping . . .

'I'm sorry.' She remembered how distressed she had been by his anger. 'But, even if what you say is true, you have no right to assume——'

'It is no assumption.' Rafaello spoke roughly. 'You want me, Jaime, just as much as I want you.'

'No——'

'What do you mean—no?' His eyes were dark with passion. 'My impatience—frightens you?'

'No. I mean—well, yes.' Jaime pressed herself against the bole of the tree. 'Raf, I want to go back.'

'Presently.'

Ignoring her anxious protest, Rafaello moved closer to her, lowering his mouth to brush the hectic swirl of colour that had come to her cheeks. Then, holding her eyes with his, he touched her mouth, and her uncertain lips parted in unknowing provocation.

'Raf——'

'Jaime!' he breathed against her mouth, silencing her, and the urgent pressure of his kiss destroyed any lingering shred of doubt.

Some minutes later he released her, and in the shining beauty of her face he found the answer he was seeking. 'Come,' he said taking her hand in his, 'we will walk,' and for the rest of the morning they tramped round the park, exchanging all the intimate facts of their existence.

Jaime told him about the break-up of her parents' marriage, of her days at school, when she had had to suffer the ignominy of parents' days when neither her father nor her mother came, and her subsequent determination to make a life for herself. Rafaello, meanwhile, spoke ruefully of his mother's disappointment that as the eldest son of the family he had not yet found a wife. He told her about his younger brother and three sisters, all of whom were married with families of their own, and his home in Italy, where his great-great-grandfather had founded a vineyard. He spoke of his own country with evident pride and affection, describing its wooded hills and ice-cold springs, its fields of rich turf, where placid cattle grazed, its mountains and streams and winding rivers, all drowsing peacefully under the warm Italian sun.

Jaime supposed she should have realised at once that their relationship was doomed. In spite of his evident love for England, Rafaello was first and foremost a product of his background, and the kind of commitment his brother and sisters enjoyed was totally alien to Jaime's principles. But she told herself that it didn't matter, that his was only a passing infatuation, and that once he returned to Italy he would forget all about her.

Of course, when they got back to the house, the

Temples' disapproval was obvious, and Jaime was sure it was only the presence of their other house-guests and the unpleasantness it would cause that prevented Mrs Temple from asking her to leave. So far as they were concerned, she had betrayed their hospitality, and Nicola refused to speak to her.

The rest of Boxing Day passed quickly. Unlike her, Rafaello had no qualms about showing how he felt, and ignoring the Temples' outrage, he gave every appearance of a man deeply in love. He had hired a car for the duration of his stay in England, and in the afternoon he took Jaime away from the dour condemnation of their hosts, driving the fifty or so miles to the coast and buying her afternoon tea at an hotel in Worthing. He behaved impeccably all afternoon, making no demands upon her, and only on the way back did his self-control falter.

'When will I see you again?' he asked, pulling the car off the road into a layby. 'You said you are leaving tomorrow. You had better give me your address, so I may know where to find you.'

With the recollection of her dingy bedsitter in the back of her mind, Jaime was less than enthusiastic. 'I—you can ring me at work,' she temporised, giving him her office telephone number. 'I don't have a telephone where I live, and—and my landlady isn't keen on anyone taking calls on her phone.'

'But the address,' said Rafaello patiently, flicking off the cap of his pen. 'I want to know where you live, not where you are employed.'

Jaime sighed. 'You wouldn't like it. Where I live, I mean.'

'Let me be the judge of that,' replied Rafaello flatly.

'Now, do you tell me, or do I have to get it from your office?'

It was Jaime's first experience of his intransigence, and with a gesture of impatience, she acquiesced. 'It's 36 Sycamore Terrace,' she told him stiffly. 'That's in Earls Court. And if you come by car, don't blame me if you get your wheels stolen!'

She had hunched her shoulders as she spoke, half turning away from him, but now Rafaello's arm came around her, drawing her back against the muscled strength of his chest. 'Do not be so aggressive, *cara*,' he breathed, his lips tracing the outline of her ear. 'I am not interested in the area in which you live, only in you.'

Somehow, her jacket was unfastened, and his palms slid possessively up over her midriff to her breasts. Feeling their sudden tautness, his hands lingered, moulding their swollen urgency, making her overwhelmingly aware of how pleasurable their touch could be.

But, as before, when his fingers probed beneath the fine wool, she lifted her hands to stop him. Rafaello, allowing her to thwart him, twisted his mouth to hers instead, and beneath the sensual probing of his kiss, her objections were forgotten. With a low sound of satisfaction Rafaello found what he was looking for, and her whole body trembled as he caressed her naked flesh.

His kisses became deeper, more passionate, robbing her of breath and resistance, arousing her to a reluctant awareness of her own sexuality. When he lifted his mouth now to seek the scented hollow at her nape, she went after him, her fingers gripping the hair at the back of his neck as her lips sought a sensual consummation.

It was Rafaello eventually who dragged himself away, smoothing back his hair with an unsteady hand. 'You see how it is between us?' he demanded, as Jaime endeavoured to slow her breathing. 'Now tell me you do not want to see me again.'

She gazed at him with tremulous eyes. 'I do want to see you again,' she admitted, stroking back an errant strand of straight dark hair from his forehead. 'Will you pick me up tomorrow night? After work?'

Rafaello was not proof against the tantalising touch of her fingers, but when her lips brushed his in open invitation, he put her firmly from him. 'Tomorrow night,' he said, tacitly accepting the fact that so long as Jaime was staying with the Temples, they could not abuse their hospitality.

During the next few weeks Jaime lived on a high of emotional excitement. For the first time in her life she neglected her studies to be with Rafaello, and their physical relationship was more satisfying than she had ever dreamed it could be.

Rafaello's discovery that she was still a virgin had both amazed and delighted him. He had, he confessed ruefully, previously been of the opinion that English girls were easy game, and to find that Jaime had never been with a man before aroused his deepest emotions. She was, he told her, everything he had ever looked for in a woman, and even though she knew messages arrived from Italy, bidding him to come home, he put off his departure time after time.

Things came to a head, Jaime remembered now, when Rafaello's mother issued the invitation for Jaime to accompany him home. She wanted to meet the girl her son found so irresistible, she said, but Jaime knew what she really wanted to do was find out whether she was suitable to be Rafaello's wife.

Up until that time, the question of marriage had been carefully avoided, on her part, at least, but suddenly it was thrust to centre stage, and she found she was no more ready to meet it now than she had been six weeks before. She cared about Rafaello, she could not have made love with him if she had not felt so strongly about him; but the idea of marriage was still anathema to her, and she had to tell him so.

The row took place in his hotel suite. During the past few weeks she had been there frequently, often meeting him at lunch time and spending the rest of the day with him, to the detriment of her job. But happily, working in the typing pool meant that there was always someone to cover for her, and the girls she worked with thought her affair with Rafaello very romantic.

And it was, thought Jaime ruefully, leaving her pillows to adopt a cross-legged position, one knee drawn up to rest her chin on. Probably none of her friends would have considered giving up an Italian count—albeit a courtesy title, these days—simply because they had this mental block concerning marital relationships. A need for independence was one thing; giving up the man one loved was quite another.

The trouble was, Jaime wasn't at all sure she did *love* Rafaello, at least, not in the way he said he loved her. Even though their physical relationship was so fulfilling, she was still haunted by the memory of what had happened to her mother, and the determination which had sustained her through harrowing days at school persistently urged her to hang on to her freedom. What did she really know of Rafaello, after all? What did she know of his way of life? And would she really be happy giving up her career for the doubtful security of a wedding ring?

Appropriately enough, it was Nicola herself who destroyed the thing she had been instrumental in starting. Jaime had arranged to meet Rafaello for lunch, but at the last minute she received a message saying he couldn't make it, that he was having lunch with his London bankers, and would she wait for him at the hotel. As it happened, Jaime had arranged to return to the office that afternoon, so that one of the other girls could go to a wedding, and in consequence she was forced to leave a message at the hotel, telling Rafaello she would meet him later.

It was almost six by the time she got to his suite, having had to stay later than she had expected, and the sudden downpour that had coincided with the rush-hour traffic had filled all the buses and taxis.

Rafaello was waiting for her, a grim brooding inquisitor, still wearing the dark business suit he had worn for lunch. Her knock brought him to the door of the suite to open it for her, but his usual kiss of welcome was absent as he abruptly turned away.

'You are late!'

'I know. I'm sorry.' Jaime was removing her wet coat as she spoke. 'Mr Forden gave me some letters to type just as I was getting ready to leave, and then— what with the rain——'

'You could not leave them, I suppose.' Rafaello faced her across the luxurious expanse of Indian carpet, his hands pushed aggressively into the pockets of his pants.

'The letters?' Jaime made a helpless gesture. 'No. How could I? It's my job.'

'And your job is important to you, is it not?'

Jaime was confused. 'Well, of course.'

'How important?'

Jaime put down her coat and moistened her lips. 'I don't understand . . .'

'I asked, how important is your job?' Rafaello incised harshly. 'More important than us? Than our relationship? Than *me*?'

Jaime blinked. 'Raf——'

'I want to know, Jaime. I have to know,' he added, with sudden emotion. 'Tell me that what I have been hearing is untrue. Tell me that this career you are making for yourself is not the most important thing in your life. Tell me that these weeks we have spent together have meant as much to you as they have meant to me.'

Jaime expelled her breath unsteadily. 'I don't understand,' she said again. 'What have you been hearing? And from whom? I thought you were having lunch with your bankers. Was that a lie?'

'No, it was not a lie.' Rafaello took one hand out of his pocket and pushed back his hair with a weary hand. Then, pacing restlessly across to the marble fireplace, he rested his arm on its mantel. 'My bankers are Clay International,' he said, turning his head to look at her. 'The representative I had lunch with was Charles Temple.'

'Oh!' Jaime began to comprehend. 'Nicola's father.'

'And Nicola,' inserted Rafaello grimly. 'She came along too.'

Jaime looked down at her hands and found they were trembling. 'And what did they say?'

'Charles?' Raf shrugged. 'Charles said nothing. What would you expect him to say? But——' he paused, 'when lunch was over, he conveniently saw a business acquaintance across the restaurant he wanted to have a word with, and I was left to entertain Nicola.'

'Instead of which, she entertained you,' exclaimed Jaime bitterly.

'Was she lying?' Raf straightened away from the mantel. 'If you tell me there was no element of truth in what she was saying, then naturally I will believe you.'

'But you have doubts, don't you?' demanded Jaime unevenly. 'You couldn't just dismiss what she said without accusing me!'

Raf's dark eyes held hers with smouldering passion. 'You know why I could not dismiss what she said,' he declared. 'For two weeks now, I have been trying to get you to agree to come to Italy with me, to meet my family, but you will not come. You prevaricate, you make excuses; and more strongly I get the feeling that you never will.'

'I can't just take time off——' Jaime began, but Rafaello was ready for her.

'Why not? What does it matter if they fire you, if you are going to marry me?'

'M-marry you?' Jaime swallowed convulsively.

'Of course. You knew this was to come,' exclaimed Raf roughly. '*Dio mio*, you cannot think, after everything we have been to one another, that I would be satisfied with anything less?'

Jaime shook her head. 'But—marriage——'

'Yes, marriage,' agreed Rafaello fiercely, crossing the room towards her. 'Oh, Jaime,' he muttered, his grip on her arms almost painful, 'tell me my fears have all been for nothing! This afternoon, I have been almost out of my mind with the agony of not knowing whether she was lying. She said you had told her you had no intention of getting married, that everyone knew how you felt but me. Tell me it is not true, and I will believe you! Tell me she was only trying to hurt you. Jaime, in the name of all the saints, say something to put me out of my misery!'

'Oh, Raf——' Jaime felt his urgent breath against her temple, and knew the almost overwhelming impulse to give in; to tell him Nicola was wrong, to promise that she would marry him, just as soon as the arrangements could be made. But she hesitated too long, and in her hesitation Rafaello sensed that Nicola had not spoken without reason.

'She was right,' he choked, drawing back far enough, so that he could look into her face. '*Dio mio*, she was right! And I, poor fool, have been trying to make excuses for you!'

'No——' Jaime put out her hands towards him, but Rafaello held her back, his face contorted with emotion.

'What do you mean—no? Are you telling me you will marry me, after all? That in spite of everything you are willing to submit?'

He almost spat the words at her, and Jaime moved her head helplessly from side to side. 'Raf, you've got to give me time——'

'Time? Time? How much time do you need to decide between your life and mine?'

'Raf, it's not like that——'

'What is it like? Tell me!' His lips twisted. 'Am I not rich enough, is that it? Were I some Brazilian millionaire, would I be looked upon more favourably?'

Jaime's shoulders sagged. 'That's not fair, Raf! You are not trying to understand——'

'Make me.'

She sighed. 'Raf, my parents split up when I was a very small girl. My father—well, my father wanted his freedom, and he didn't much care what happened to us. My mother had to scrape and save to make ends meet.'

'So?' Rafaello shook his head impatiently. 'What has this to do with you and me?'

'You're not making it easy for me——'

'Why should I?'

Jaime bent her head. 'You don't know what it's like—having no money——'

'You went to a good school,' he reminded her.

'Only because a cousin of my mother's took pity on us,' exclaimed Jaime bitterly. 'I—I swore then that—that no man would ever do that to me——'

'You think I would?' Rafaello caught her shoulders and dragged her round to face him.

'I—don't know, do I?'

'*Cristo*——'

'Rafaello, my parents were in love when they got married, really in love. My mother told me so. She—she was at college. She wanted to be a teacher. My father was in the Army, and he wouldn't wait. She left college because she was expecting me.'

Rafaello raised his eyes heavenward. 'Jaime, that was more than twenty years ago——'

'Has anything changed?' Jaime looked up at him tensely. 'A woman is still vulnerable, Raf. Marriage makes her vulnerable. Children make her vulnerable. I need time——'

'No!'

'No?' Jaime trembled. 'I don't understand——'

'Oh, I think you do.' Rafaello was pale. 'There is no more time. I have listened to what you have to say, and I tell you, I will not wait any longer. I regret what you have told me. I regret what happened to your mother. But I do not see what that has to do with us.'

'Raf, I'm like my mother, don't you see? I have a chance for a career, too——'

'As a typist!' He was scornful.

'To begin with, yes.' Jaime held up her head. 'But I don't intend to remain a typist all my life. The course I'm taking at college——'

'Oh, spare me the details!' Rafaello was savage. 'Do you think I want to hear about your *job*? You are a fool, Jaime, and you have made a fool of me, too.' He gazed at her contemptuously. 'I could kill you for that!'

Jaime was frightened now. Not because of his threat to kill her; she would almost have welcomed his violence. Her fear was of a deeper kind, of a more fundamental nature, a realisation that perhaps she had been wrong, after all.

'Raf—please!' she begged. 'Don't be like this. I do care about you, *I do*! But you're asking too much, too soon——'

'Or not enough,' he snapped fiercely. 'Perhaps you

would have preferred me to ask you to live with me. Is that the kind of relationship you had in mind?'

Jaime shook her head. 'We were together—that was enough.'

'For you, perhaps.' He clenched his fists. 'What kind of a woman are you?'

'Raf, you're not trying to see it my way. And—and I can't bear it when you treat me like this.'

'So?' he snapped fiercely. 'How would you have me treat you?' His mouth thinned. 'Are you asking me not to waste this golden opportunity?'

'What do you mean?' Jaime took a step back from him now. 'Raf?' she questioned uncertainly, and then caught her breath when his hands clamped on to her shoulders and his meaning was very plain.

'You just said it,' he declared. 'You said you cared about me. Well——' his bitter gaze swept her from head to foot, 'that is something I can understand.'

Jaime gulped. 'Raf, don't—don't look at me like that! I'm trying to be civilised about this.'

'Oh, so am I,' he retorted harshly. 'Completely civilised. And what could be more civil but that we part the way we came together? As lovers!'

'Raf!' Jaime gazed at him disbelievingly. 'Raf, we have to talk about this——'

'There is no more time for talking,' he stated grimly. 'I have talked too much as it is. Obviously you understand actions, not words.' He jerked her roughly towards him, his mouth seeking the startled parting of hers. 'Why should I not take advantage? This is *all* you came here for, is it not?'

'Raf, don't——' Jaime's balled fists pressed against his chest, but he was so much stronger than she was, and he had the advantage of anger to force his will upon her.

'Relax, Jaime,' he muttered, grasping a handful of her hair and pulling her head back. 'This is what you wanted. I am only here to oblige.'

Her protests went for nothing. Beneath the imprisoning pressure of his hands, she had little chance of resistance, and besides, as his mouth continued to devour hers, the will to be free of him diminished. But as if realising he was making it easy for her, Rafaello changed his tactics. Instead of caressing her lips with warmth and tenderness, his mouth hardened to a savage assault, crushing her lips against her teeth and bringing the taste of blood to her tongue.

'Raf, you're mad——' she gasped, when she got her mouth free, but her panic only seemed to fire the fuels of his passion. With a triumphant cry he swept her up into his arms, and in spite of her flailing limbs, he carried her into the adjoining room and flung her on the bed.

Watching him as he threw off his jacket and waistcoat, tearing his shirt apart so that the buttons flew in all directions, Jaime felt he was a stranger to her. Was this how her mother had felt, she wondered, when her father changed from the charming boy she had married into the sullen man who was not averse to delivering a blow should she disobey him? Rafaello was acting in a way she would never have dreamed he could act, and when his fingers went to the belt of his trousers, she was shaken into belated action.

On trembling knees, she scrambled for the far side of the bed, but already she had waited too long. With a muttered oath he lunged on to the bed after her, and her desperate attempt was thwarted by the breath-taking weight of his body.

'Oh, no,' he said, grasping the neck of her office blouse and tearing it open. 'You have tormented me for the last time, Jaime. Now I will give you something to remember me by.'

He disposed of her clothes without care for their appearance, tossing them carelessly on to the floor as his hands took possession of her body. With infinite pleasure, he imprisoned her hands above her head, so that she could not interfere with his enjoyment, and her eyes that only minutes before had pleaded for his forgiveness spat fire for his insensitivity.

'Do you want me to hate you?' she choked, twisting beneath him, but Rafaello's face held no compassion.

'Better hatred than the puny emotion you have been nurturing,' he declared savagely. 'At least hatred has fire and passion!'

Her struggles were to no avail and, in spite of everything, Jaime began to feel a traitorous warmth in the pit of her stomach. His hands, savagely possessive as they were, were gradually arousing the feelings he had always been able to arouse, and seeing the sudden emotion in her face, Rafaello swore angrily.

'*Cagna! Lupa!* You cannot be enjoying this!' he protested violently, and Jaime dragged her swimming senses back from the brink of insanity.

'Let me go, Raf, please!' she pleaded, renewing her struggles, and Rafaello, content that she was aware of his contempt, laughed tauntingly.

'So distrait! So angry!' he jeered scornfully. 'But so desirable, I fear . . .'

His mouth left her lips to follow the creamy curve of her breast, searing a trail of burning kisses that made her flesh cringe. Finding the rigid peak, he paused briefly to suckle at its sweetness, and then, with a casual flick of his tongue, his lips moved lower to tease the quivering flatness of her stomach.

'Raf, you can't!' she choked, when his head moved even lower, and as if tiring of his game, he came astride her.

'So?' he accused tormentingly, 'why do you look so distressed? Why should I not satisfy my lust with you? Is this not what you have been doing with me?' His lips twisted. 'A fitting humiliation, is it not?'

'Raf, you can't be serious——'

'But I am.' His face was pale with emotion. 'Why should I not have you one more time? Can you think of a better way to destroy the memories that haunt me? Except by treating you as the selfish bitch you really are?'

Jaime groaned. 'Raf, don't do this——' she begged, but he was not listening to her. Uncaring that he might hurt her, he thrust himself upon her, forcing his way into her body with a savagery Jaime could not withstand. 'Oh, Raf!' she sobbed, as his urgent mouth sought the parted sweetness of hers, and her tears ran between their lips in salty protestation.

Yet, as if even in his fury he could not deny his feelings, the violence of his assault did not continue. Within the yielding warmth of her body, his movements became even, rhythmed, and his mouth that had sought hers in anger gentled to a passionate fervour. He was not raping her, she thought wildly, he was making love to her, and her own limbs responded to the feverish hunger of his embrace.

It was all over much too soon, but even then Rafaello did not draw away from her. Instead, he lay with his face buried in her hair, its silky length strewn in sensual abandon across the satin coverlet.

It was Jaime who moved first, and at her tentative stretching of her legs, Rafaello opened his eyes. She didn't know what she had expected to see in his eyes, but not the look of bitter loathing that crossed his face before he dragged himself away from her. With a groan of disgust, he got up from the bed, and snatching up his strewn clothes, he strode towards the bathroom.

'Raf——' she had to speak, but when he glanced back at her over his shoulder, she wished she hadn't.

'Go,' he commanded. 'Get out of here! When I come back, I want you to be gone!'

Looking back, Jaime thought it was the invitation to Nicola's wedding that had hurt her most. Perhaps, if Rafaello had left, if he had gone back to Italy and married some unknown Italian girl, she might have been able to dismiss him from her thoughts. Though that was unlikely. But for him to turn to Nicola, to *marry* Nicola, when she knew he had never had any intention of doing so, filled her with a terrible kind of torment. No doubt that was what he had intended, she acknowledged. It wasn't only a woman scorned who possessed that kind of cruelty. But what troubled her most was how much it hurt, how much she suffered because of his actions, and how long it took for her to come to terms with the decision she had made.

Going to the cathedral had been a deliberate attempt

to turn the knife, to kill whatever it was insid.... .t still threshed and tore at her emotions, a.. part.. it had worked. Rafaello was married now... the.. was nothing she could do about it; and she had... ft the cathedral silently, long before the brid. a... groom emerged from signing the register. It... .ver. She was free. And if that freedom had a .o..ow sound, time would quickly fill the void. An.. it had. Her work, and her success, had been bot.. a satisfaction and a fulfilment, and it was no use... w letting long-buried emotions destroy her hard..von detachment. She had done with the past. She had exorcised the ghosts that no longer came to h... .t her, and she had to learn to face Rafaello withou.. .motion, or leave here before it was too late.

CHAPTER SIX

THE tentative knock that disturbed her contemplation brought Jaime back to the present with a start. Someone had obviously seen where she had gone, she thought with sudden anxiety. She should have known that Rafaello would not be prepared to wait for her to speak to him on her own terms.

'Who is it?' she called, getting half off the bed, only to sink weakly back again when a feminine voice answered her.

'*É Lucia, signorina. Mi scusi, ma può venire?*'

Hesitating only a moment longer, Jaime got off the bed and opened the door. 'I'm sorry,' she murmured apologetically. 'What did you want?'

'*Il pranzo, signorina.*' Lucia sighed, seeking the words. 'The meal—he is ready.'

'The meal?' Jaime was confused. 'What meal?' And then, glancing disbelievingly at her watch, she knew. It was nearly one o'clock! Long past the time when Rafaello had asked to speak to her. 'Lunch?'

'*Si, signorina.*' Lucia was relieved. 'Lunch,' she repeated gratefully. 'You will come, *per piacere?*'

'Oh—yes.' Jaime put up a nervous hand to her tumbled hair. 'Just give me five minutes—er—*cinque minute?*'

'*Cinque minute,*' agreed Lucia, and with a polite bob of her head, she went away.

Left to herself, Jaime stared at her reflection with

wry misgivings. Like it or not now, Rafaello was going to be angry that she had ignored his summons, and it would give him another reason for resenting her audacity in coming here.

Her brush restored the silken strands to order and securing her hair at her nape with a leather clasp, Jaime left her room. She found her way downstairs with confidence now, her long legs covering the distance with more determination than enthusiasm, running lightly down the marble staircase, only to come to an abrupt halt in the hall below. Rafaello was just emerging from a room to the right of the stairs, and when he looked up and saw her, their glances met and clashed in mutual antipathy.

Jaime's gaze fell first, her eyes moving away from his dark face in unwelcome contrition. She didn't want to feel guilty, but she did, and lifting her shoulders offhandedly, she said: 'I didn't realise it was so late.'

'But it is,' retorted Rafaello harshly. 'Much too late. Shall we go in to lunch? My—wife is waiting for us.'

Jaime moistened her dry lips. 'Nicola? She's better?' Her eyes widened in surprise, but Rafaello showed no such emotion.

'Oh, yes,' he replied, gesturing for her to precede him. 'Nicola has a healthy appetite, you will find.' He paused before adding in a faintly sardonic tone: 'For someone whose nerves are so fragile.'

Nicola was waiting at the table, her fingers drumming impatiently against the cloth. Her eyes narrowed slightly when her husband and Jaime appeared together, and her first words were an uneasy reminder of why she had brought Jaime to the Castello.

'So there you are, Jaime,' she exclaimed, her gaze skimming her husband's dark face to settle on the other girl's somewhat troubled features. 'Where did you go? We were having such a cosy conversation. Just because I felt unwell——'

'I—I had a headache,' murmured Jaime uncomfortably, taking the chair Rafaello was holding out for her. 'I—went to my room, and I'm afraid I forgot the time.'

'I see.' Nicola's eyes shifted back to Rafaello as he seated himself at the end of the table. 'I thought you might have been together.'

'I see you are feeling much better,' inserted Rafaello, as one of the maids came to serve them. 'As usual, you are looking for a reason to blame someone else for your own shortcomings.'

'Raf!'

Nicola's cry of protest brought an unwilling surge of sympathy, and Jaime concentrated hard on the tiny slivers of fish on her plate. Anchovies, olives, mushrooms, tomatoes—she had little appetite for any of the food, and Rafaello's harsh denunciation did not make it any easier to swallow.

Yet, in spite of her husband's derision, Nicola made a good meal, blandly consuming everything that was put in front of her. From time to time, inadvertently on her part at least, Jaime's eyes encountered Raf's and she was quick to look away from their inimical appraisal. It was as if he knew exactly what she was thinking, and although he didn't say anything, his meaning was implicit. No one who had been so violently sick less than two hours ago should have made such a rapid recovery, and even though Jaime

Yours **FREE** with a home subscription to

SUPEROMANCES™

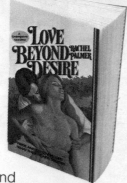

Now you never have to miss reading the newest **SUPEROMANCES**... because they'll be delivered right to your door.

Start with your free *Love beyond Desire.* You'll be enthralled by this powerful love story...from the moment Robin meets the dark, handsome Carlos and finds herself involved in the jealousies, bitterness and secret passions of the Lopez family. Where her own forbidden love threatens to shatter her life.

Your free *Love beyond Desire* is only the beginning. A subscription to **SUPEROMANCE** lets you look forward to a long love affair. Month after month, you'll receive four love stories of heroic dimension. Novels that will involve you in spellbinding intrigue, forbidden love and fiery passions.

You'll begin this series of sensuous, exciting contemporary novels...written by some of the top romance novelists of the day...with four every month.

And this big value...each novel, almost 400 pages of compelling reading...is yours for only $2.50 a book. Hours of entertainment every month for so little. Far less than a first-run movie or pay-TV. Newly published novels, with beautifully illustrated covers, filled with page after page of delicious escape into a world of romantic love...delivered right to your home.

A compelling love story of mystery and intrigue… conflicts and jealousies… and a forbidden love that threatens to shatter the lives of all involved with the aristocratic Lopez family.

┌─ **Mail this card today for your FREE gifts.**

EXTRA BONUS
MAIL YOUR ORDER
TODAY AND GET A
FREE TOTE BAG
FROM SUPERROMANCE.

Mail this card today for your FREE gifts.

knew Nicola had not feigned her illness, she felt she was missing some significance in the other girl's behaviour.

When the fish plates had been removed and a dish of cold meats had taken their place, Nicola made another attempt to start a conversation. Adopting a conciliatory tone, she said lightly: 'We must try and make your visit interesting, Jaime. There's very little to do here, but we are within driving distance of Florence and Siena, and the coastline is quite pretty, if you don't mind the crowds.'

'Oh, really——' Jaime protested nervously, 'there's no need to entertain me. I—er—well, I'm quite happy doing nothing, you know. I have—quite an active life in London, and it's a chance to relax . . .'

'You must not forget that—Jaime—probably does quite a lot of travelling in the course of her work, Nicola,' remarked Rafaello, but Jaime did not like his tone. 'After all, we are fortunate that she has found the time to visit us. We must not presume to monopolise her freedom.'

Nicola's smile was smug. 'I'm sure if you offered to show Jaime your country, she would not refuse, Raf.' And ignoring the other girl's shocked intake of breath, she continued: 'I know you didn't part the best of friends, but can't we forget about the past?'

Rafaello's mouth thinned. 'What are you suggesting, Nicola? That I neglect my work at this most important time of the year?'

'Oh, please——' Jaime began, but she was not allowed to finish.

'Why not?' Nicola demanded. 'Carlo Priori is

perfectly capable of looking after your precious vines for a few days.'

'So that I may escort you two ladies on a conducted tour of Tuscany?' Rafaello's nostrils flared. 'I think not, Nicola. I am not a tour guide. I am quite sure you will find Lorenzo Costa far more satisfactory.'

Nicola held up her head. 'I don't want Lorenzo Costa.'

Rafaello shrugged. 'That has not been my impression.'

Nicola put down her fork. 'What's that supposed to mean?'

'Whatever you care to make of it, Nicola,' replied Rafaello smoothly.

Nicola's fists clenched. 'You—you bastard!'

'It is not I who is the *bastardo*, Nicola.'

'How—how can you?'

Nicola almost sobbed the words, and Jaime wanted to die of embarrassment. 'If you'll excuse me——' she started, only to be interrupted again, this time by Rafaello.

'It is I who ask to be excused, signorina,' he declared formally, pushing back his chair. '*A più tardi.* I will see you both at dinner.'

Rafaello's departure left an uncomfortable void that Nicola seemed in no hurry to fill. For a while she seemed absorbed with her thoughts, but after a bowl of huge Italian strawberries had been set before her, she ventured an explanation.

'Raf's so—jealous,' she exclaimed, and her careless words turned an unwelcome knife in Jaime's stomach. 'Oh, he doesn't care about me, about how lonely I am, but if I—if I make a friend of anyone . . .'

'Like Lorenzo Costa,' murmured Jaime unwillingly,

and Nicola nodded vigorously.

'You've met Lorenzo. You know how—charming he can be. And he's been so—kind to me.'

'Kind?' Jaime was sceptical.

'Yes, kind,' declared Nicola defensively. 'I think if it wasn't for Lorenzo, I'd have gone quietly mad!'

Jaime shook her head. 'But is it wise? Antagonising Raf, I mean? If he objects to your friendship——'

'Oh, I knew you'd take his side,' muttered Nicola tearfully. 'You're not trying to understand.'

'I am trying, Nicola.' Jaime wished she could be more objective about it. 'It's just that—well, I don't see how my being here is going to help matters.'

'It won't. If you refuse to help me,' Nicola retaliated resentfully. 'Have you thought about what I asked you earlier? You saw how impossible it is for me to speak to Raf. Couldn't you at least make an effort?'

Jaime got up from the table now, pushing her annoyingly unsteady hands into the pockets of her jeans. She had known this was coming, and she was still unable to answer her. How could she speak to Rafaello? How could she plead Nicola's case? How could she ask anything of him, when he had so obviously not forgotten or forgiven the past?

'Nicola——'

'I know what you're going to say, and I won't accept it,' the other girl stated fiercely, pushing back her chair. 'Raf will listen to you, if he'll listen to anyone. Please, Jaime, don't let me down! You're the only person I can trust.'

Jaime was relieved when Nicola told her she was going to rest after lunch. 'I still feel a bit queasy,' she confessed, although how she could after what she had just eaten, Jaime did not know. However, it did give Jaime the opportunity to have time to collect her thoughts, and when Nicola had gone upstairs, she stepped out into the blazing heat of the afternoon.

A somnolent haze lay over the castle. Even the birds' song seemed muted in the still air, and the buzzing insects were the only active things that she could see. Across the river below her, cattle grazed lazily in the lush green pasture, and the occasional car that passed on the road to Vaggio seemed to be moving at a snail's pace.

Jaime sighed. If only her thoughts could respond to their surroundings! Instead, her brain was whirling from trying to come to terms with her situation, and her blood still ran hotly after giving in to that bout of retrospection. It was no use telling herself that the past was dead when it still had the power to disturb her. Emotions were like embers; once stirred, they flared into faltering life, and she had to take care they did not consume her in their flames.

She prepared for dinner that evening with real reluctance. The memory of the scene between Rafaello and Nicola she had been forced to witness at lunchtime was still uppermost in her thoughts, and she dreaded another confrontation over dinner. Perhaps she could make some excuse for not joining them, she pondered, as she took a cooling shower, but the realisation of how futile this would be quickly doused her enthusiasm. After all, she had come here to help Nicola, not to shy away at the first obstacle.

She dressed in a pair of clinging silk pants that moulded her long shapely legs. To go with them there was a sleeveless tunic, with side lacings and a narrow gold belt that accentuated the full curve of her breasts. The colour, a deep shade of violet, flattered the faint tan that already glowed on her face and arms, and a dark mascara gave her eyes a silvery gleam. Her hair presented the most problems. It was too warm an evening to leave its weight loose about her shoulders, but she was bored with keeping it in its coil at her nape. Instead she secured the silken strands in a single braid, looping it behind her ear, where gold circles cast their own lustre.

It was a little after a quarter to eight when she went downstairs, her pulses quickening unwillingly at the sight of lamplight spilling from the open doors of the library. This was a scenario she had never expected to have to play out, and although she told herself it was only nerves, she was uneasy.

She halted at the doorway to the library, looking inside with some trepidation. Walls of books formed a backcloth for a heavy oak desk and two high-backed armchairs, but in spite of the tray of drinks residing on a polished cabinet, the room appeared to be empty. She was about to turn away when one of the armchairs turned on its axis, and as she watched, Rafaello rose from its worn leather depths and came towards her. In a dark red velvet dinner jacket, he was once again the detached individual who had met her at Pisa airport, and the muscles of her face stiffened as his chilling eyes appraised her.

'Can I offer you a drink?' he enquired, and accepting his unspoken invitation, Jaime stepped reluctantly into the room.

'Campari, thank you,' she acknowledged, linking

her slightly damp fingers together. 'I—where's Nicola? Isn't she down yet?'

'My wife will not be joining us.' Rafaello put down his own glass to attend to Jaime's requirements. 'Would you like soda?'

'Just a little.' Jaime caught her lower lip between her teeth. 'Er—is Nicola all right? She's not been sick again?'

'Not to my knowledge,' affirmed Rafaello coolly, handing her a tall glass. 'I am sorry if my undiluted company is a bore to you. I will endeavour to avoid any embarrassing topics.'

Jaime pressed her lips together, taking the glass from him but making no attempt to taste the liquid it contained. 'I'm sorry,' she said tightly. 'It's I who should apologise. I had no idea my coming here would cause so much unpleasantness.'

'Did you not?' Rafaello had retrieved his glass and now stood, resting his hips against the desk. 'Oh, I am pretty sure you knew exactly how much unpleasantness your coming here would cause. And I wish you to leave as soon as possible.'

Jaime caught her breath. 'Was that what you wanted to say to me this morning?'

'Among other things,' conceded Rafaello bleakly, bowing his head. 'However, you chose not to listen to my feelings in the matter. Consequently, I am forced to tell you in the plainest words possible.'

Jaime felt suddenly angry. Here she was, trying to make excuses for being here, to a man who was treating her as if she had wanted to come. Rafaello should at least respect her honesty. Or had he become so immured to lies, he couldn't recognise the truth when he heard it?

'I think you've said quite enough,' she exclaimed, steeling herself to face his wrath. 'I don't like being here any more than you like my company. I can think of a dozen things I'd rather be doing right at this moment!'

'And with someone else,' Rafaello interrupted her scornfully, so that Jaime completely lost her temper.

'Yes, if you must know,' she retorted hotly. 'I'm used to being treated as an equal, not as an inferior. You may get away with that with Nicola, but you won't get away with it with me! No wonder she came to me, begging for my help and my support. My God, you're an anachronism, do you know that? You stand there, laying down your laws, and expect everyone else to fall over themselves to obey you!'

Rafaello's features were rigid, and for a moment she feared he intended to do her some physical harm. He took an involuntary step towards her, froze into an attitude of dark menace—and then, as if compelled by some inner force, he turned away.

'Another drink?' he offered stiffly, careless of the fact that she had not even tried the Campari that she held, and Jaime expelled the breath, she had unknowingly been holding, to shake her head.

'No. I mean—this is fine,' she muttered, finally making an effort to swallow the liquid. 'Thank you.'

The maid's arrival to announce that dinner was ready was hardly a diversion. Seated in the dining room, alone with Rafaello at the table, Jaime wished she had known Nicola would not be joining them. But apparently the other girl had no qualms about leaving her husband and her friend together, and it was left to

Jaime to wonder exactly what she expected her to say. Whatever it was, Jaime knew she had little hope of appealing to Rafaello's better judgment this evening. She had successfully destroyed what little chance she might have had of convincing him of her impartiality, and looking at him now, she wondered how Nicola had ever expected she could.

When the plates containing the main courses had been removed and a dish of fruit and several varieties of cheese had been set before them, Rafaello chose to break the uneasy silence between them.

'This cheese is produced not far from here,' he declared, forking a creamy-white cube on to her plate. 'Cheese is an important part of an Italian meal, as witness its addition to soups and pastas, and of course, as it is now, with good wine and—good conversation.'

Jaime cast a wary look in his direction. 'You're joking, of course.'

'You do not find the wine to your taste?' His dark eyes were enigmatic. 'It is from our own vineyards, a vintage I have long been fond of.'

'I wasn't talking about the wine, and you know it,' said Jaime unsteadily. 'Oh, what am I supposed to say? That I'm sorry? That I was rude? I was, I know it. But you get me so—so——'

'Angry?'

'Frustrated,' declared Jaime helplessly. 'You won't listen to reason. You make your own interpretation of the situation, and you refuse to be moved from it.'

'So——' Rafaello poured himself more wine, and then raised the glass towards her. The lamplight glinted on cut glass and dark red wine, and cast shadows over his taut features. 'We will call a truce, hmm?

You may keep your secrets and I will keep mine. But for now, we will forget our differences and discuss the impersonal things that two people who have not seen one another for so many years might discuss.'

Jaime expelled her breath. 'Can we do that?'

'We can try,' he averred, his tone hardening slightly. He swallowed his wine. 'Come, we will have coffee in the library, then Maria can clear the table.'

Ensconced in an armchair in the library, Jaime felt no less on edge. The truce, such as it was, was a fragile thing, and she couldn't help remembering how violent Rafaello's anger could be. She could only hope to divert him from their differences, for tonight at least, and tomorrow, if Nicola was still adamant, she would have to think of some new way to approach him.

In fact, the remainder of the evening was not unpleasant. Released from the necessity of finding ways of combating Rafaello's hostility, Jaime found it increasingly easy to talk to him. With the barriers of the past put aside for a few hours, it was not difficult to discuss her work and the cosmetics industry in general, touching briefly on their plans for the future, which included Martin's idea of promoting a line of clothes to complement their product.

'Mary Quant did it,' she explained, 'and other manufacturers have followed suit. What we would hope to achieve is a Helena Holt image; clothes, make-up; hair, too, if we can manage it. There's even talk of moving into masculine territory, with a range of clothes and cosmetics suitable to Helena Holt's male counterpart.'

Rafaello shook his head. 'Paris Holt, one would assume,' he remarked dryly, and Jaime looked blank.

'Helen of Troy,' he explained mockingly. 'It was Paris who eloped with her, wasn't it?'

'Oh——' Jaime gurgled with laughter. 'I hadn't thought of that. But no. Somehow, I can't see boys going for the Paris look! I thought something more like Knight-errant or Paladin. Paladin, preferably. Something short and recognisable, and totally masculine.'

'Why not Stag or Toro—they are short enough for you, are they not?'

'But not very subtle,' said Jaime ruefully.

'No.' Rafaello bent his head. 'Subtlety was never my strongest suit.' His dark eyes flickered briefly over her face. 'Can I offer you another drink?'

'Oh—no, thank you.' With a determined effort Jaime got to her feet, stepping back abruptly when he followed her example. 'I think—I think it's time I went to bed. I am rather—tired. It's been a—long day.'

'An unusual day,' conceded Rafaello, with a tight smile. 'I have enjoyed our conversation, Jaime. It is obvious why you are so successful in your job, why you like it so much. I doubt any man could hope to compete.'

But lying awake much later Jaime wondered why what he had said no longer seemed so entirely convincing. She did enjoy her work, she was proud of her achievements, and until coming here, she had had no self-doubts.

She sighed. Perhaps it was not so unnatural that she should question her convictions here, when she had been thrown into the company of the one man who had ever threatened her beliefs. There was little use in labouring the point that if she had known what Nicola had expected of her, she would not have come. Nicola had been desperate, and suicidal. How could Jaime have ignored her appeal, in whatever terms it was couched? Rafaello's involvement had seemed inevitable, but no way could she have guessed exactly what had gone wrong with their marriage. She pushed her fist into the pillow in an effort to make herself more comfortable, and determinedly prepared herself for sleep. Tomorrow, she thought, with grim resolution, tomorrow she would find a way to broach Nicola's demands . . .

But she didn't.

When tomorrow dawned, warm and sunny and full of expectation, it brought with it a message from Rafaello, inviting her to a tour of the vineyard. 'If you are interested,' the note Lucia delivered ended, and Jaime guessed he half expected her to refuse.

'Er—*vorrei venire*,' she told the maid, groping for the few words of Italian she had picked up from a phrase book. '*Grazie.*'

'*Di niente, signorina.*' Lucia smiled and departed, and Jaime hastily scrambled into her clothes.

Downstairs, the smell of freshly-brewed coffee drew her to the dining room, but as on the previous morning, it seemed she was to breakfast alone. Only Maria hovered about the table, putting the finishing touches to a neatly-folded napkin and adjusting the gleaming silver cutlery to her satisfaction.

'Ah, *buon giorno, signorina*,' she greeted Jaime with some warmth. '*Il conte* says you will eat something before you leave. You wish anything more?'

Jaime surveyed the table helplessly. With a dish of rolls warming over a flame, and curls of creamy butter residing beside some of the delicious conserve she had tasted the day before, she could think of nothing she would enjoy more.

'This is fine, Maria,' she affirmed, smiling at the old woman. '*Molte grazie.*'

'*Prego, prego,*' Maria assured her with evident relief, and Jaime couldn't help wondering how Nicola could have alienated these friendly people.

'Count di Vaggio?' she queried, as Maria made for the door. 'He—won't be joining me?'

'*Il conte,* he have breakfast an hour ago, *signorina,*' Maria replied apologetically. '*Salute.*'

Jaime did enjoy the meal. It had been the one period of the previous day when she had been allowed to eat in comfort, without the ever-present awareness of her hosts, and she did not fool herself that today would be any different. In consequence, she was still sitting over her second cup of coffee when Rafaello appeared, but for once he did not greet her with his usual aggression.

'You ride?' he enquired, after offering a formal salutation, and Jaime was too bemused to prevaricate.

'A little,' she admitted, realising that was the meaning of his casual attire, and Rafaello expelled his breath with satisfaction.

'Then—if you are ready?' he invited, gesturing towards the door, and smoothing her palms down over the seams of her narrow-legged jeans, Jaime acquiesced.

The animal Rafaello had chosen for her to ride was called Elsa. She was a beautiful chestnut mare, long-limbed but docile, he assured her, springing into the saddle of the black stallion Lorenzo had told her about the day before. An elderly groom had held the mare's head while Jaime swung herself on to its back, and she was relieved that the arrogant chauffeur was not a knowing witness to her ineptitude.

'Relax,' said Rafaello, as they moved out of the stable yard. 'You are holding the reins as if you expected them to be torn from your grasp. I have told you, Elsa will not alarm you. She is too old to—how do you English say it?—learn new tricks, no?'

Jaime grimaced. 'I'm not sure whether I like that or not,' she exclaimed, allowing her knees to relax their grip only fractionally, and Rafaello's lazy smile appeared.

'What? Would you have had me mount you on Raffica or Diabolo?'

'If Diabolo means what I think it means, then no!' declared Jaime fervently. She looked about her with more confidence. 'How far is it to the vineyard? Do you always go on horseback?'

'Sometimes yes, sometimes no,' he admitted, allowing Primato his head. 'Come, we go this way. I will show you the land my ancestors fought and died to retain.'

The morning passed much too quickly. It was years since Jaime had been on a horse, and although she suspected she might feel stiff the next day, she soon lost all feeling of nervousness. In no time at all she was encouraging Elsa into a canter, and fretting a little impatiently when the placid creature refused to respond as energetically as she could have wished.

In the woods below the castle, the air was still sharp and crisp, but out on the slanting hillside, the sun soon disposed of the dew sparkling on the grass. A track led through the woods and down to where terraces of vines formed a living shelter for their juicy burden. Acres of the grape-producing plants spread their mantle over the sloping ground, tended by a handful of workers, whose job it was to ensure that no pest or plant disease struck the vines before harvesting could take place.

'Did you know it is the carbon dioxide in the air that penetrates the leaves of the vine and ultimately provides the sugar from which wine is derived?' Rafaello asked as, after tethering their horses, they walked along the rows of growing plants. 'See,' he added, pointing to the burgeoning fruit on the stem, 'it is important that the grapes are not permitted to absorb too much sugar before they are picked. To be successful, it is necessary to keep a constant check on the levels of glucose, and something called fructose, in the fruit. Nowadays, thank goodness, it is possible to use modern technology to achieve the required result. It was not always so easy.'

Jaime was intrigued. 'I suppose you don't tread the grapes any more either,' she teased, as they emerged near the storage sheds, and was rewarded by Rafaello's attractive smile.

'Regrettably not,' he conceded, looking down at his booted feet. 'But if you were here at harvest time, I might be able to——'

Jaime looked away from the sudden, and uni-dentifiable, emotion that darkened his eyes as he broke off. The moment was charged and dangerous, and to escape the unwelcome racing of her pulses, she went into the nearest storage shed, wrinkling her nose at the stale atmosphere. The shed was empty at present, a few empty casks all that remained of the previous year's vintage, and she took a few deep breaths to dispel a more bitter image.

'We should go back.'

Rafaello's voice behind her brought her round with a start, and she put an involuntary hand to her throat as she glimpsed his harsh expression in the gloom. 'What you mean is—we shouldn't,' she responded, pushing past him, and for once the brilliant sunlight did not have the strength to warm her.

CHAPTER SEVEN

'So what did you talk about?'

It was later that day, and Nicola had cornered Jaime after lunch and insisted she accompany her on a shopping trip into Vaggio su Ravino. Now, they were seated in the little tea-rooms overlooking the small square of the town, and Nicola was presently forking the last morsel of Jaime's unwanted pastry.

'Oh—this and that.' In all honesty, Jaime was finding it difficult to remember exactly what they had talked about, and her conscience was not eased to discover that Nicola showed no obvious trace of jealousy. On the contrary, the other girl seemed well pleased that Rafaello had apparently changed his mind, and although she must have been disappointed that Jaime had not taken advantage of her opportunities, she had not reproached her for it.

'I suppose it must be strange for you and Raf to spend time alone together,' Nicola ventured now, summoning the waitress to order another pastry. 'I mean—after all these years.' She paused. 'I knew he wouldn't be able to resist you.'

'Nicola!' Jaime felt the blood rushing up under her skin, but the other girl only shrugged.

'Don't look so shocked, Jaime. I'm not suggesting there's been any indiscretion——'

'I should hope not!'

'—but you have to admit you still find Raf attractive, don't you?'

'For goodness' sake, Nicola!' Jaime glanced impatiently round the small restaurant, but the other girl only made a resigned grimace.

'Well, it's true,' she exclaimed. 'Just because you've chosen to deny your femininity, it doesn't mean you've taken a vow of chastity, Jaime.'

'No, it doesn't.' Jaime drew a deep breath. 'But nor is my life so devoid of human relationships that I need to turn to another girl's husband for consolation!'

'Oh, Jaime!' Nicola accepted a sugared confection, oozing with cream, on to her plate. 'I'm not suggesting you'd consider having an affair with Raf. I'm just being realistic, that's all. Anyway,' she licked her lips delicately, 'if you and Raf do become friends, just think how much easier it will be for you to talk about me.'

Jaime cupped her chin on her knuckles. 'You really are convinced that I can persuade Raf, aren't you?'

'If anybody can,' the other girl agreed.

'And if he refuses to talk about it?'

'You'll find a way.'

'Nicky, I may not be able to.'

Nicola's attention was briefly distracted from her plate. 'If you care about me, you'll do it.'

Jaime shook her head. 'It isn't a question of caring.' She halted and then went on more slowly: 'When was the last time *you* tried to talk to Raf?'

'I don't know.' Nicola poured herself more tea. 'Yesterday; last week; what does it matter? I've told you——'

'I can't believe he's so intractable——'

'Oh, can't you?' Nicola's lips twisted. 'How would you know? Have you asked him?'

Jaime sighed. 'Nicola, listen to me——'

'No, you listen to me.' Nicola leant tensely towards her. 'I'm afraid, Jaime. I half believe Raf only married me to punish me.'

'That's ridiculous, Nicola!'

'Is it? Is it? I sometimes think he doesn't care about me at all.'

Jaime lay back in her chair, defeated, and Nicola consumed the remainder of the pastry. 'I suppose you think I eat too much, too,' she remarked, wiping her fingers on a napkin. 'Well, you know what they say about eating to compensate.'

Jaime's shoulders moved in a helpless gesture. 'It won't help if you start putting on weight, will it?'

Nicola's eyes flashed. 'I'm not putting on weight. I haven't lost my figure yet!'

'Lost your figure?' Jaime sighed. 'No, of course you haven't lost your figure, but——'

'He won't want me if I'm fat!'

'All I'm saying is——'

'All you're saying is that I should go on and on giving in to Raf's selfishness,' declared Nicola, through tight lips. 'Could you do it? Could you be content with my life?'

Jaime bent her head. 'We're not talking about me.'

'No, we're not.' Nicola sniffed. 'But perhaps we should. Perhaps we should probe the reasons why you're so unwilling to help me.'

'Nicola!'

Jaime met the other girl's eyes indignantly, and as if she realised she had gone too far, Nicola's expression changed. 'Oh, I'm sorry, I'm sorry,' she exclaimed, her narrow fingers fastening round Jaime's wrist. 'I didn't mean that—I didn't. I know you're only thinking of me. But you don't know what it's like, day in and day out.'

Jaime pushed back her chair and got to her feet. 'I'm not making any promises, Nicola.'

'But you'll think about it.'

'I already am,' replied Jaime flatly, walking towards the cashier's desk.

Dinner was a subdued meal that evening. Jaime guessed Nicola was endeavouring not to create any more disturbing situations, and Rafaello seemed absorbed with his own thoughts.

When the meal was over, however, he did have one announcement to make before he left the two girls to their coffee. 'Mamma telephoned this afternoon,' he declared, addressing himself chiefly to his wife. 'I invited her to spend a few days with us while—Jaime is here. As she knows the area as well as I do, I thought you might welcome her as my replacement, as I have to go to Rome tomorrow.'

'No!'

Nicola was on her feet before he had finished speaking, and then, as if realising her protest could be misconstrued, she added: 'I mean, we'll come to Rome with you, Raf, Jaime and I. I—I'm sure we'd both enjoy——'

'I think not.' Rafaello shook his head sombrely. 'You invited Jaime here for a holiday, Nicola. I do not think the hot streets of my nation's capital are exactly what she had in mind.'

'Don't be silly.' Nicola glanced impatiently at the

other girl. 'Raf, you can't expect Jaime to welcome your mother's company—she's an old woman!'

'Nicola, honestly . . .' Jaime had to intervene, though not, she feared, in the way her friend had intended. 'I—I shall look forward to meeting Signora di Vaggio. Please, don't concern yourself on my account.'

The look Nicola flashed her then was one of wild desperation. Her clear blue eyes glittered with unshed tears, and Jaime, returning her stare helplessly, began to suspect she had underestimated the state of Nicola's imbalance. Until then, she had not realised how precariously drawn the other girl's nerves must be, but all of a sudden Nicola's threats of self-destruction did not seem so unbelievable.

'Nevertheless,' said Rafaello, apparently indifferent to his wife's distress, 'the arrangements have been made, and we will adhere to them. It is time you started to consider someone other than yourself, and Mamma has been very patient with you in the past.'

Nicola's lips trembled. 'I don't want her here! I don't want that lying old woman here! She hates me, you know she does. Why do you do these things to hurt me?'

'To hurt you?' Rafaello's voice had an edge of ice. 'You do not know the meaning of the word!'

'Oh, please——' Jaime could see Nicola was visibly swaying now, and she was very much afraid that Rafaello's anger would drive her friend over the brink. 'I'm sure Nicola didn't mean what she said. She's upset, that's all—distraught! I'm sure if——'

'Keep out of this, Jaime!' Rafaello snapped the words as he strode towards the door. 'You are not one of the family! You have no right to interfere in matters which do not concern you. Please keep your opinions to yourself. You know *nothing*!'

The door slammed behind him, and watching Nicola as she subsided into her chair, Jaime wondered which of them felt the worst. Nicola was quivering, it was true, and her fingers clasped and unclasped with the intensity of her emotions, but the drained feeling Jaime was experiencing could hardly be surpassed. She felt sick and dizzy, stunned by the pain of his rejection, and weak with the knowledge that he could inflict such agony unheedingly.

'It's no use, it's no use . . .'

Nicola's groan of despair alerted Jaime to an awareness of where she was and what was happening. Whatever her own feelings, it was Nicola's feelings she should be concerned with, and gathering her strength, she endeavoured to speak calmly.

'What's—no use?' she asked, forcing a note of optimism to her voice. 'Nicola, you mustn't let these arguments upset you. All—all married couples have their differences. And besides, Raf's mother can't be that bad.'

'She is, she is.' Nicola's jaw trembled. 'She hates me!'

'Oh, don't be silly. Mothers-in-law don't hate their sons' wives. They may not—approve, exactly——'

'Approve!' Nicola rubbed her nose with a shaking finger. 'You don't know, Jaime, you don't know. She's a terrible woman. She'll turn you against me, too.'

'She won't. What are you saying?' Jaime found talking was easier than thinking. 'Are you trying to tell me that it was Raf's mother who turned him against you?'

'Yes! Yes!' Nicola sniffed miserably. 'Oh, Jaime, what am I going to do? If Raf's in Rome and you're here, how are you ever going to be able to talk to him?'

Jaime moistened her lips. 'He won't be in Rome for ever, will he?'

'You mean—you'll stay?' Nicola grasped her hands and stared at her through wildly tearful eyes. 'But I thought—you said——'

'Yes, well——' Jaime hesitated, already half regretting the impulse which had made her offer to stay on. 'I could stay another week——'

'A week?' Nicola gulped. 'Oh, Jaime, you don't know how grateful I am! Wait until Raf finds out. He'll be so—so——'

'—furious?' enquired Jaime flatly, the sickness she had succeeded in dispelling returning to plague her, but Nicola shook her head.

'No,' she said quickly. 'Why should he be? He asked his mother here for your sake.' Her lips twisted. 'Or so he said.'

'Yes—well——' Jaime got to her feet, suddenly desperate to get away from Nicola, away from Raf, away from this room which had seen the disintegration of her belief in herself. 'I'm tired, I'm going to bed. I'll see you in the morning.'

Nicola watched her leave, an expression of relief having taken the place of her previous hysteria, and Jaime envied her her ability to change moods so swiftly. Looking at Nicola now, it was almost impossible to believe that only minutes before she had been swaying on the edge of an emotional precipice. Now it was Jaime who could feel the narrowness of the

path she was treading, and the instability of her
position seemed unlikely to improve.

Rafaello's mother arrived in the early afternoon. She
drove herself in a huge, outdated Mercedes, that
nevertheless succeeded in retaining its air of power
and elegance.

Jaime might not have witnessed her arrival had it
not been for Lorenzo Costa. She had decided to go for
a walk after lunch, when Nicola said she was going to
rest, and the handsome young chauffeur had encountered her in the courtyard and offered his escort.

'No strings,' he declared humorously, holding up
his hands, when Jaime's expression questioned his
integrity, and glad of the distraction, she had agreed.
The disturbing trend of her own thoughts had long
begun to weary her, and it was with a sense of relief
that she gave herself up to his uncomplicated
companionship.

Leaving the castle behind, they climbed a slope
starred with daisies and bluebells, to where a spring
burst out of the hillside. Around the stones nearby
mosses clung, making the way slippery, and Jaime
kicked off her sandals and dipped her feet into the cool
water. From here it was possible to view the whole
sweep of the valley, and she perched on a ledge and
drew up her knees.

'You look—anxious,' remarked Lorenzo quietly,
adopting a squatting position beside her. 'Is something
wrong? You seem—intense. Are you not enjoying your
holiday, after all?'

'What?' Jaime glanced his way quickly. 'Oh—oh,
yes.' She had no wish to get involved with personal

relationships again. 'I was just admiring the view. It's quite spectacular.'

'Quite,' he agreed, quirking a dark eyebrow. 'And *il conte* is king of all he surveys.'

Jaime refused to take the bait, and instead pointed to the undulating curve that wound away into the hills to their right. 'That's the road to Santo Giustino, isn't it?' she commented. 'There's a beautiful cathedral at Santo Giustino. But I suppose you know that, having lived here all your life.'

'How do you know where I have lived all my life?' Lorenzo countered quickly. 'Did Nicola tell you? Did Nicola talk about me?'

'Nicola?' Jaime repeated the name to give herself time to think. 'I—why, no.' She paused. 'Why should you think she might?'

Lorenzo shrugged. '*Bene*, she could hardly talk to *il conte*, could she?'

'Why not?' Jaime knew she ought to go no further with this, but Lorenzo's complacency was infuriating. 'What couldn't she talk to—to the count about?'

'Why, the cognac I get for her, of course, *signorina*,' he declared blandly, but Jaime had the distinct impression that was not what he meant.

Shaking her head, she rested her chin upon her knees, wondering as she did so why Lorenzo's attitude towards Nicola troubled her so much. After all, if Rafaello suspected there was anything between his wife and the handsome chauffeur, he would have dismissed him long ago, and it was obvious from Lorenzo's behaviour that he did not think this was imminent. The man was over-confident, that was all, but likeable with it, she decided, else why had she agreed to his company herself?

'You have a job in England, *signorina*?' he asked now, subsiding on to the grass and resting back on his elbows. 'Let me guess: you are a *modella*, no?'

'I'm a model, no,' agreed Jaime drily, giving him a sideways glance. 'As a matter of fact, I have an office job. Nothing exotic, I'm afraid.'

'Ah . . .' Lorenzo nodded, 'that is a shame. You would make a good model, I think.'

'So would you,' retorted Jaime crisply, and Lorenzo's laughter was loud and spontaneous.

'I think, perhaps, you are a feminist, *signorina*,' he exclaimed sobering. 'Is that why you have never married? I cannot believe no man has ever asked you.'

'How do you now I haven't been married?' Jaime responded, using his own argument against him. 'And divorced? I may have been, for all you know.'

'This is true.' Lorenzo lifted his shoulders in acknowledgment. 'But I do not think you have been married, *signorina*. A lover, yes. Perhaps, more than one. But no husband.'

Jaime pushed herself to her feet, controlling her colour with the utmost difficulty. The last thing she needed was to be reminded of her affair with Rafaello, and Lorenzo's eyes were too intent, too knowing. It crossed her mind that perhaps he had suspicions, too, and it was this as much as anything that prompted their return to the castle.

So it was that Jaime and Lorenzo entered the courtyard just as the Dowager Contessa di Vaggio was emerging from her car. A small woman, somewhat overweight in middle age, Rafaello's mother neverthe-less possessed a formidable presence, and her dark eyes alighted instantly on the two young people still flushed from the exertion of their walk. Jaime was taken aback by the expression of hostility that crossed Rafaello's mother's face as she took in their somewhat dishevelled appearance, and her nerves tightened uncomfortably at the unwelcome notion that the older woman knew exactly who she was. It was possible that she should remember, Jaime thought with some trepidation. After all, Rafaello had wanted them to meet. But if his mother resented that previous relationship as much as he did, then in God's name, why had Rafaello invited his mother here at this time?

'It is—Signorina Forster, is it not?'

In the few seconds Jaime had taken to ponder this new development, the Dowager Contessa di Vaggio had left her car to approach them. Lorenzo, with a polite inclination of his head that included both women, swiftly made his departure, and it was left to Jaime to face this redoubtable little woman alone.

'I—yes, *contessa*,' she answered, wondering why she felt the urge to curtsey. 'Er—how do you do? Did you have a good journey?'

'I enjoy driving,' Rafaello's mother agreed, without warmth. 'So—we meet at last.' She held out her hand. 'You are not at all as I imagined you.'

Jaime expelled her breath weakly. 'I'm sorry.'

'Do not be.' The older woman's brows arched above well-fleshed yet patrician features. 'My thoughts of you were never charitable, *signorina*. But I am bound to say that Rafaello did not exaggerate your beauty.'

'Thank you.'

Jaime did not know what else to reply, but the Dowager Contessa only shrugged. 'It was not a

compliment, *signorina*. I was merely commenting on
the reasons for Rafaello's infatuation. An infatuation
that ruined his life, I might add, and for which he is
still paying!'

Before Jaime could make any response to this
damning pronouncement, the Contessa turned away,
and ignoring the girl's open-mouthed indignation, she
summoned Giulio to take her bags.

'*Comé sta?*' she enquired, following the servant into
the castle. '*Dov'è la signora?*'

Jaime followed more slowly, unwilling to be
involved in Nicola's reception of her mother-in-law.
But she had to admit her friend was right: Rafaello's
mother evidently disapproved of her son's choice in
women.

To her relief, there was no sign of the visitor when
she entered the hall. Giulio had no doubt taken his
erstwhile mistress up to her apartments, and abandoning her tentative idea of examining the books in
Rafaello's library, Jaime followed suit.

In her own room, however, it was not so easy to
dismiss thoughts of the new arrival. Rafaello had left
that morning for an unspecified stay in Rome, and she
very much suspected that his decision to invite his
mother to the castle was simply another way to tell her
to leave. After all, he must have known how his
mother would react to her, and if Jaime had any sense
at all, she would go now before she got any deeper into
this mess. But she couldn't leave Nicola, not without
making some effort on her behalf, and it crossed her
mind swiftly that perhaps Rafaello's mother might be
more sympathetic than her son. Surely she must want
a grandchild from her eldest son? Rafaello used to say

so. Jaime shivered. She had once considered providing that child herself . . .

Dinner was to be served at eight o'clock, as usual, and Jaime prepared for the meal, with even less enthusiasm than on previous evenings. Meeting Rafaello's mother again in Nicola's presence was not going to be easy, and determined not to let the older woman intimidate her again, she deliberately dressed in a bronze silk tailored pants suit. She had bought the suit on her last trip to Paris, and it was recognisably cut by a master hand, and with it she wore a matching silk shirt and a flowing buttercup yellow tie. She also coiled her hair severely back from her face, to expose her delicate bone structure, using a subtle eye make-up to hide the evidence of her disturbed nights. Examining her reflection before she left her room, she thought she looked cool and sophisticated, and ever-so-slightly masculine, unaware that the sensuous swell of her breasts pressing against the fine silk of her shirt and the unconscious sway of her hips left no one in any doubt as to her gender. Even so, she did achieve part of her objective, which was to convince Rafaello's mother she had found the success she had sought at his expense.

After her outburst of the night before, Nicola was politely subdued, but her eyes widened at Jaime's immaculate appearance. In a creamy-coloured cocktail dress, glittering with rhinestones, she was the feminine foil for her friend's Amazonian elegance, and Jaime wondered if Rafaello's mother was wondering how her son could have been attracted to two such disparate females.

This evening, the Contessa was dressed in black, her swarthy skin enhanced by a glittering diamond necklace. She looked every inch the matriarch she was, and during dinner she lost no opportunity to make her presence felt. The servants evidently deferred to her, as the senior member of the family, and although this was quite understandable, Jaime thought that if she was in Nicola's position, she would not allow the old woman such free licence. But Nicola seemed indifferent to her mother-in-law's presumption, and it was only as they were leaving the table that Jaime thought she understood why. Nicola had been drinking; the scent of alcohol on her breath was out of all proportion to the single glass of wine she had consumed with the meal, and the slightly glazed appearance of her eyes bore witness to a drugging quantity of some other spirit.

Ignoring Jaime's gasp of impatience, Nicola shook off her friend's detaining hand and followed her mother-in-law across the hall to the library. But after ensuring that the tray of coffee was waiting for them, she asked to be excused for a moment, and fifteen minutes later Jaime came to the conclusion that Nicola was not coming back.

'You do not have to stay, *signorina*,' Rafaello's mother remarked, after Jaime had looked towards the door for the umpteenth time. 'Go: do what you wish. I shall be quite content here. I have brought my sewing, see? It is an old woman's pastime, and one which someone of your intelligence would not wish to emulate.'

Jaime expelled her breath on a sigh. 'Why do I get the impression that my—quotes—intelligence—close

quotes—is not something you regard in a compli-
mentary light, *contessa*?'

'Did you get that impression, *signorina*?' The older
woman bent to extract a white linen cloth and a
handful of embroidery silks from a bag beside her. 'It
was not intended as a criticism, merely a statement of
fact.'

'I have sewn, in the past,' Jaime commented briefly,
despising the impulse to defend herself to this woman.
'When I was young, *contessa*, my mother and I often
made our own clothes.'

'Indeed?' Rafaello's mother smoothed out the cloth
she had taken from the bag and studied the design.
'You surprise me, *signorina*. I should have thought you
might have found some other way to dress yourself.
Are the men in England blind?'

Jaime caught her breath. 'That's an offensive thing
to suggest,' she exclaimed, annoyed to hear the
betraying tremor in her voice as she spoke. 'I don't
know what you're accusing me of, *signorina*, but girls
in my country do not usually sell their bodies for the
sake of ambition! My mother and I were poor, it is
true. After my father left us, we did not find it easy to
make ends meet. But to my knowledge neither of us
was desperate enough to take to the streets!'

The vehemence of her denial must have made some
impression on Rafaello's mother, for when Jaime
would have risen to her feet, the Contessa put a
detaining hand on her sleeve. 'Wait, *signorina*,' she
said tautly. 'I am sorry. I should not have said what I
did, and I ask you to forgive me. You must put it
down to an old woman's anxiety for her son. It is hard
for me to forgive you, but as Rafaello appears to have

done so, I must at least try.'

Jaime moistened her dry lips. 'I—I don't know what you mean.'

'Oh, I think you do.' Rafaello's mother assured herself that Jaime would not leave if she released her, and cut off a length of scarlet silk. 'You cannot pretend that the past never happened. It did—I have Rafaello's word for it. And the certain knowledge that had you not walked out on him, he would not now be suffering the results of his reactions.'

Jaime's legs felt like water—with a comparable strength. It was just as well she had remained in her chair, she thought weakly. She doubted they had the ability to support her. But her brain was still active, and her tongue, and choosing her words carefully, she replied:

'I did not walk out on Raf, *contessa*. He walked out on me.'

'What nonsense is this?' The older woman looked up from her work. 'Are you calling my son a liar, *signorina*? He told me himself that you refused to marry him.'

'Oh—well, yes. Yes, I suppose I did that,' admitted Jaime unevenly. 'But that's not the same as——'

'To my son it would be,' declared the Contessa stiffly. 'We are a proud family, *signorina*. Are you suggesting Rafaello should have agreed to live with you without the blessing of the church?'

Jaime bent her head. 'I knew he wouldn't.'

'So you chose to punish him for being an honourable man.'

'It wasn't like that.' Jaime looked up. 'You don't understand, *contessa*. I wanted to be independent. I wanted to prove I was as capable of providing for myself as any man. And I have proved it. I have a good job, a good career——'

'—and no love!' inserted Rafaello's mother harshly. 'I wonder—was it worth it? Five years on, would you still do the same?'

Jaime schooled her features. 'I—think so.'

'Then you are a fool!' The Contessa's needle attacked the cloth with angry strokes. 'I see now what my son saw in you—why he wanted you, instead of that faithless creature upstairs. You have pride and integrity; you would not betray your principles and choose the easy way out; but you are a fool, nevertheless. And sooner or later you will realise it!'

CHAPTER EIGHT

IN spite of their differences, Jaime found her feelings towards Rafaello's mother gradually mellowed over the next few days. Because Nicola chose to remain in bed most mornings until lunchtime, Jaime was thrown much into the company of the elderly Contessa, and not wanting to exacerbate the situation, she was obliged to make an effort to be sociable. She did not approve of the way Nicola was behaving, and she lost no opportunity to tell her so, but the other girl seemed determined to appear in the worst light possible, and it was left to Jaime to try and justify her behaviour.

Although she had not put much faith in Rafaello's assertion that his mother would act as courier should she wish to see more of Tuscany, the old Contessa herself offered to take Jaime wherever she wanted to go. 'You do drive, do you not, *signorina?*' she enquired, when she first broached the subject, and as Jaime's reply was positive, she nodded her head equably. 'Good. Then you can act as chauffeur,' she declared, settling the matter. 'I drive when I have to, but only then. I much prefer to be a passenger.'

'I'm sure Lorenzo——' began Jaime, getting ready to suggest that perhaps her son would be more inclined to approve of his own chauffeur than herself, but the Contessa's dark eyes glittered.

'I would not permit that young man to drive me anywhere,' she declared, before adding scornfully:

'But if you should prefer it——'

'Oh, no.' Jaime was not going to be caught in that trap. 'I only thought——'

'Where Lorenzo Costa is concerned, I would advise you not to think,' the old lady stated grimly. 'Now, where shall we go for our first outing?'

In the event, they went to Siena, spending the morning visiting the cathedral and the art gallery, and the Palazzo Pubblico, where they climbed the tower to get a view of the surrounding districts. Jaime liked Siena. She liked the town and she liked the people; and most of all she liked the architecture and the magnificent works of art which had made Siena famous.

Nicola was indifferent to her enthusiasm when she got back. 'How you can spend so much time with that horrible old woman, I'll never know,' she declared, after Rafaello's mother had retired for an afternoon *siesta*. 'I intend to telephone Raf and ask him when he plans to come back. I refuse to go on being treated like a visitor in my own home!'

Jaime, flushed and pleasantly tired after her morning in the sun, stretched slim bare legs on the couch in the *salotto*. This small sitting room opened on to a small patio that in turn gave on to the terraced gardens below the castle, and since the Contessa's arrival it had been used for relaxing after meals. 'I think you ask for everything you get,' she said now, trying to be fair. 'After all, you don't make any effort to get on with her, do you? And as for allowing her to order the servants about—well, you don't seem interested in household matters.'

'I've told you, the servants turn against me,' Nicola

muttered resentfully, but Jaime shook her head.

'I think you turn them against you,' she countered gently. 'You obviously don't like them, and you let them know it. If you——'

'So you've turned against me, too!' Nicola burst out tearfully. 'I wondered how long it would take. What has that old witch been saying to you? What has she been telling you about me? It's lies, all lies. She always hated me, always!'

'Calm down, calm down!' Jaime was perturbed and showed it, swinging her legs to the floor and regarding the other girl anxiously. 'I haven't turned against you, Nicola. Don't start that again. I'm merely pointing out that you haven't exactly endeared yourself to your mother-in-law, have you?'

'Why should I?' Nicola pushed her hands into the pockets of the baggy coveralls she was wearing, going to stand with her back against the frame of the french windows. 'I know what she thinks of me. I know that if divorce was possible in their religion, she'd encourage Rafaello to seek his freedom.' Her lips tightened as she turned to give Jaime a curiously feline look. 'But divorce isn't acceptable,' she declared, not without a certain amount of satisfaction. 'And the marriage could hardly be annulled when I've had one miscarriage, could it? No,' her lips twisted, 'Raf's stuck with me. And the sooner he accepts that, the better.'

Jaime could feel every nerve in her body tighten. 'What do you mean?' she asked, disturbed by the sudden malevolence in Nicola's tone. It was almost as if she was gloating over something, although what Jaime couldn't imagine.

'It doesn't matter.' Evidently Nicola had decided she had said enough. 'I'm going up to my room. Why don't you join me? I've got something there that will definitely brighten this boring afternoon.'

'No, thanks.' Jaime remained where she was, sickened by Nicola's obvious indifference to everything she had been saying, and the other girl shrugged.

'Suit yourself,' she said, sauntering towards the door. 'But don't blame me for being the way I am. Blame that self-righteous bastard I married. Blame him for the mess I've got myself into now!'

Jaime looked up at her. 'What mess?'

Nicola avoided her eyes. 'What do you think?'

Jaime shook her head. 'You mean—your drinking?'

Nicola grimaced. 'What else?' she countered bitterly, and wrenching open the door made her exit.

During the days that followed, Jaime drove Rafaello's mother all over the northern part of Tuscany. They went to Empoli and Certaldo, and Poggibonsi, famed for its wine, and the ferry port of Piombino, gateway to the island of Elba. But Jaime's favourite place was Florence, the centre of European civilisation for hundreds of years, and home of some of the greatest works of art ever commissioned. The full day they spent there could not begin to encompass the scope of its churches and museums, its palaces and art galleries. Jaime thought she would like to spend at least a week wandering through its streets and squares and winding alleys, and remembering the way Rafaello used to talk about his homeland, she began to appreciate the love he had for it.

It was during the day they spent in Florence that Jaime attempted to talk to the Contessa about her daughter-in-law. She was in a state of some elation, having spent the afternoon touring the Uffizi Gallery, and when Rafaello's mother suggested finding a *caffe* where they could buy a cup of tea and she could rest her aching feet, Jaime seized the chance of holding her attention.

'What a pity Nicola isn't with us,' she ventured, using her own enthusiasm as an excuse to bring Nicola's name into the conversation, but the Contessa refused to take the bait.

'I do not think I have walked so much since Tonio grew out of his *carrozzina*—his baby state, you know,' she admitted, rubbing the toes of one foot against the ankle of the other. 'But I have enjoyed it, Jaime. And I am grateful to you for that.'

'Oh, please——' Jaime shook her head, relieved that her attempt to introduce Nicola's name had not encouraged the Contessa to revert to her previously formal address of *signorina*. For two days now, she had been Jaime to her companion, and their relationship had warmed accordingly.

But it was useless to pretend that Nicola did not exist, and taking another deep breath, Jaime took a second plunge. 'She's not a happy girl, you know,' she tendered, stirring her tea with more vigour than necessity. 'I wish you would try and understand her position, Contessa. She desperately wants to do the right thing.'

'You think that?' Rafaello's mother's eyes flashed impatiently. Then, as if realising their association had gone beyond the bounds of mere acquaintances, she added more feelingly: 'I do not want to quarrel with you, Jaime. These past days—they have been pleasant for me, more pleasant than I could have imagined. Do not spoil them by talking about Nicola. She is not your concern. Regrettably, she is Rafaello's, and Rafaello's alone. It is up to him to decide what must be done about her.'

'What must be done about her?' Jaime blinked uncertainly. 'I'm afraid I don't understand.'

'But you know what is wrong with her, do you not?'

Jaime's tongue circled her lips. 'What is wrong with her?' she echoed, playing for time, and the Contessa's thin lips drew down at the corners.

'Do not lie to me, Jaime. You have been here—what? A week? Eight days? Surely in that time Nicola has confided in you, in her best friend?'

Jaime shook her head. 'Perhaps.'

'So.' Rafaello's mother shrugged her shoulders. 'What more is there to say?'

'You mean—Raf knows too?'

'Do you doubt it?' The Contessa gazed at her aghast. 'My child, my son may be many things, but he is not a fool. Of course he knows. I imagine the whole castle knows.' Her fingers gripped the edge of the table. 'I will never forgive my husband. Never!'

'Your husband?' Jaime had the feeling she was losing the threads of this conversation. 'I'm afraid I don't see what your husband has to do with it? He died so long ago.'

'The sins of the fathers,' declared Rafaello's mother bitterly. 'You know that saying, I am sure. It was never more true than in this context.'

Jaime sipped her tea helplessly. Evidently, the Contessa thought she saw some connection she did not. But whatever the outcome, she had to make one final effort on Nicola's behalf. 'Don't you think,' she suggested, 'Raf might give her another chance?'

'Another chance?' The Contessa snorted angrily. 'What are you saying? That Rafaello should forgive and forget? Oh, no, *signorina*, you ask too much. When—when the child died, he might have forgiven her then, but she was not content. She had only herself to blame for the result.'

Jaime bit her lip. 'But is it so wrong to want a baby?' she exclaimed. 'I should have thought you——'

'You ask *that*!' The Contessa stared at her in contempt. '*Dio mio*, take me home, *signorina*. I do not wish to discuss the matter again.'

Rafaello arrived home that evening.

Jaime could have wished he had chosen some other evening to return to the castle. The atmosphere between the three women was decidedly chilly, and she was sorry about that after the pleasant few days she and the Contessa had spent. But no doubt Rafaello would have been suspicious if he had returned to find his mother and Jaime the best of friends, so perhaps it was fortuitous anyway.

During dinner, he spoke almost exclusively to his mother, and Jaime told herself she was relieved. But after the meal was over, he did not retire as he usually did, joining Jaime and his mother in the *salotto* for the ritual pouring of the coffee.

Nicola, who had been silent throughout dinner, joined them, too, seating herself on a pale green buttoned sofa, and accepting the cup of coffee her mother-in-law handed to her with carefully-assumed politeness. All evening she had been throwing malevolent glances at the old lady whenever she was not looking, catching Jaime's eye with mocking indifference, involving her in a situation that was far from transparent; but now she sat there demurely, like a child at a special treat, her innocent appearance belying what lay underneath.

'Was your trip successful?' she enquired, after they were all seated, and Jaime held her breath. Nicola must have heard her husband discussing a meeting he had held with his accountant with his mother, yet she was behaving as if nothing had been said.

'Reasonably,' Rafaello responded now, his dark face sombre above the ruffled front of his cream shirt. It was obvious he was loath to continue with that particular topic, and as if understanding this Nicola changed her approach.

'We've missed you,' she said, causing the Contessa's cup to rattle against her saucer. 'Jaime was just saying yesterday how empty the castle seemed without you. It was a pity you had to go away, just as you and she were getting to know one another again.'

Jaime didn't know who was the most embarrassed—Rafaello, the Contessa, or herself. And it was patently untrue that she had made such a statement; Nicola knew that as well as she did. So why was she telling such barefaced lies when they could only alienate the situation still further?

'I think you exaggerate, Nicola,' Rafaello said at last, his nostrils flaring. 'I am sure Miss Forster said nothing of the kind.'

'Why are you calling her Miss Forster?' Nicola's eyes widened ingenuously. 'You always call her Jaime, you know you do. It would be rather foolish to call her anything else after what you two have been to one another.'

'*Nicola!*'

'*Nicola!*'

Jaime and Rafaello spoke simultaneously, but Nicola was undeterred. 'Don't look so shocked. We all know I'm telling the truth. Where's the harm? I'm not suggesting there's anything between you now.'

But she was, Jaime knew that. By adopting this attitude, Nicola was choosing the only sure way she had of insinuating a relationship that she knew did not exist. And while Rafaello's mother might have baulked at an outright accusation, this apparently innocent innuendo suggested just the right measure of complicity. Jaime could tell by the Contessa's expression that she was troubled by Nicola's behaviour, and although Rafaello was more adept at hiding his feelings, his anger at his wife's conduct was evident in the tautness of his features.

'Anyway,' Nicola smiled, content with the reactions she had evoked, 'you're home now, and that's all that matters, isn't it?' She finished her coffee and put down her cup. 'Mmm, that was delicious, Mamma, but I think I'll go up to my room now—I'm rather tired. Goodnight.'

Her departure was achieved in silence, and after the door had closed behind her, the ominous absence of sound continued. But then, as if she, too, was suddenly tired, the Contessa also rose to her feet.

'We will talk again in the morning, Rafaello,' she said, speaking in English for Jaime's benefit. But as he sprang to open the door for her, saying: 'Mamma——'

in a rather driven tone, she placed a reassuring hand on his sleeve.

'*Capisco, capisco,*' she murmured, her expression taut with feeling. '*Non ha importanza.*'

'No?' Rafaello shook his head. '*Buona notte, Mamma.*'

'*Buona notte, figlio mio. Buona notte, Jaime.*'

Jaime stood up as Rafaello closed the door. 'I suppose I'd better leave too,' she murmured, smoothing the skirt of the simple cream chemise dress she was wearing. 'I'm sorry if what—Nicola said embarrased you or your mother, but——'

Rafaello rested his back against the door, successfully cutting off her means of escape. 'It did not embarrass you?' he asked tightly, pushing his hands into the pockets of his velvet jacket. 'My wife's insinuations that you had some personal motive for desiring my return? You were not offended?'

Jaime's blood ran a little faster. 'No.'

'No?'

'No.' She crossed her arms protectively across her midriff. 'You know it wasn't true. And I'm sure your mother was not deceived. Nicola was just—playing games, trying to—trying to——'

'——divert attention from herself, perhaps?' Rafaello's tone was harsh. 'Mamma tells me you are staunch in her defence.'

Jaime's brows drew together. 'Your mother? I——'

'We spoke earlier,' he explained tersely. 'Before you came down to dinner.' He paused. 'She also tells me you and she have spent much time together these last few days.'

'Oh—yes.' Jaime could feel her stomach muscles

tightening. 'She has been very kind.'

Rafaello's dark eyes appraised her. 'That was not what she said,' he observed. 'Mamma was of the opinion that you had taken pity on her.'

'Oh, no!' Jaime was fervent. 'I—we—our outings were of mutual enjoyment, I think. She is a very likeable person.'

Rafaello moved away from the door. 'Nicola did not accompany you.' It was a statement rather than a question and Jaime merely shook her head. 'I am told she spent most mornings in bed.'

Jaime gasped. 'Do you have her watched?' she exclaimed indignantly. 'Surely she——'

'I do not have her watched,' snapped Rafaello in response. 'But you must understand, there are people in the castle who waste no time in telling me of my wife's activities while I am away, do you take my meaning?'

'You shouldn't listen.'

'You cannot be serious.' Rafaello pushed frustrated fingers into his hair. 'Do you think I should reveal that these things trouble me?'

'Then Nicola was right; the servants do dislike her.'

Rafaello sighed. 'The servants do not dislike her, Jaime. They simply have no respect for her.'

'And whose fault is that?'

Rafaello's eyes darkened angrily. 'Are you suggesting that it is mine?'

'Well, isn't it?' Now that she had started, Jaime had to go on. 'I mean——' she took a deep breath, 'wouldn't Nicola's position here be more secure if she—if she had children?'

Rafaello covered the space between them with

frightening speed, staring into her startled eyes with sudden loathing. 'You mean that?' he demanded contemptuously. 'You would put me in that position, without a shred of compassion?'

'A shred of compassion?' Jaime stood her ground bravely. 'You married her, didn't you? You made her your wife! Doesn't that entitle her to some rights in this supposedly religious country? Or is that kind of loyalty reserved for the church and the holy fathers who administer it?'

Rafaello's face was suffused with anger. 'How dare you?' he choked. 'How dare you speak to me of loyalty?'

'She's your wife, Raf. She had your child! Shouldn't that mean something?'

'Yes!' said Rafaello, between his teeth. 'It should mean something. It *did* mean something. But have you never asked yourself why I married Nicola?'

'I assumed——'

'Yes? What did you assume, I wonder? Did you think perhaps that I fell out of love with you and into love with Nicola in the space of a few weeks?'

'Well——'

'Or perhaps you thought I married her to get even with you, that I had condemned myself to a life of bondage for the sake of making you jealous!'

'I——'

'Did you even imagine that perhaps I had never loved you at all? That my feelings for you were as *shallow* as your feelings evidently were for me?'

'Raf——'

'It was none of those things!' he told her savagely, his hands clenched at his sides. 'I had no desire to marry Nicola! I had no interest in marrying anyone. Indeed, that night you left the hotel, my strongest feelings were of self-disgust, and self-contempt, that I should have allowed any woman to so dictate my actions! I despised you, Jaime. But I despised myself still more. You had made me do what I did, you had reduced me to an—an animal, motivated only by rage and jealousy. You were the reason I had abandoned every honourable code! But I was to blame, for being so deceived.'

'Raf——' She would have turned away, but his hand on her shoulder prevented it.

'You will listen to me,' he stated grimly. 'You will hear what I have to say. Then you will decide which of us is guilty.'

Jaime quivered. 'Is there any point?'

'I think so.' He drew a deep breath. 'To go on: the night you left the hotel, I was desperate. Self-hatred is the most destructive kind and robbed of the will to destroy myself one way, I proceeded to do it another.' He paused. 'Alcohol helped, but it was no real opiate. I was still conscious when Nicola telephoned, still capable of telling her that you and I were through.'

'Nicola?' Jaime stared at him, and Rafaello nodded heavily.

'You did not know? I thought not. Well, your— friend—rang to find out how successful her little ploy had been. She was very clever. She asked to speak to you. I, of course, was in no state to deny that you were not with me.'

'Even so——'

'Wait!' Rafaello's fingers dug painfully into her bones. 'When she discovered you were apparently out of the picture, she rang off. Fifteen minutes later she was at my door.'

'No!'

'But yes.' Rafaello sighed. 'Oh, do not be misled. Nothing happened—nothing of a physical nature, that is. I was not—how do you say it?—capable of gratifying her in that way. But her father was not to know that.'

'Her father?'

'Regrettably, yes. Someone—you may guess who— had advised him of his daughter's whereabouts. When Charles arrived at the hotel, Nicola chose to be found in a state of some undress. The outcome was inevitable.'

'But——'

'At the time, I did not care,' exclaimed Rafaello harshly. 'I suppose I could have denied everything, but my brain simply refused to function. In no time at all the marriage was arranged. It was what Nicola wanted. I thought it was what my mother wanted. And as you and I——' He broke off abruptly, his free hand descending on her other shoulder to hold her in an agonising grip. 'Perhaps there was an element of revenge in it,' he muttered thickly. 'Perhaps I did get a certain satisfaction from knowing it might hurt you. But I was wrong, was I not? You did not give a damn!'

Jaime's breathing quickened. 'Raf——'

'Answer me, damn you!'

'I—I—I can't,' she choked, her voice breaking. 'I can't!'

'Why can't you?' Rafaello's dark eyes were smouldering with some unidentifiable emotion. 'Are you going to lie to me again? Are you going to tell me you might have changed your mind? Are you going to tie my guts in knots by suggesting you regretted leaving me?'

'I—I didn't leave you, Raf——'

'What would you call it?'

'I said I needed more time.'

'An excuse!'

'It wasn't.' Jaime licked her dry lips. 'I—I don't know what I'd have done. After you ordered me out of the hotel——'

'After I raped you, you mean? After I destroyed the only decent thing there had been between us?'

'You didn't rape me,' moaned Jaime, in a tortured voice. 'You know you couldn't go through with it. You—you made love to me. You always made love to me.'

'As I want to make love to you now,' he muttered harshly, his eyes moving hungrily over her face. 'As I have wanted to make love to you ever since I saw you at the airport——'

'No, Raf——'

'Yes, Raf,' he contradicted grimly. 'Is that not the admission you have wanted to hear?'

'No——'

'But you came here knowing how it would torment me——'

'No. Nicola invited me.'

'And why do you think Nicola invited you, if not to torment me?'

'Raf, Nicola is desperate!'

'As am I,' he told her hoarsely, his hands sliding over her shoulders. 'As am I, Jaime.'

She turned her face away from his, but his lips slid

along her cheekbones, arousing an unbearable sense of recognition. His hands probed her shoulderbones, finding the little hollow beside her spine, and as she was compelled closer, she felt his teeth against her earlobe.

'Do not fight me, Jaime,' he groaned, his breath stirring the silky strands of pale hair at her nape, and she felt her senses swimming at the well-remembered feel of his taut body.

'Raf——' she began, half turning her face towards him, but her protest was useless. Moving swiftly, he captured her anxious face between his hands, and her troubled words were stifled by his hungry possession.

Time receded while his mouth reacquainted itself with the parted contours of hers. His lips were warm and passionate, searching and probing and awakening emotions inside her that she had never thought to have awakened again. She wanted to resist him, she wanted to push him away from her, and break that urgent contact before any irreparable damage was done. But her hands and lips betrayed her; the burning urgency of his passion was all-consuming, and her hands groped for the hair at the back of his neck, grasping and holding and clinging to him desperately.

'Jaime——' he said against her mouth. 'Oh, Jaime, why did you have to come here?'

It was no easier to make the break, but Rafaello's broken words tore Jaime apart. She had no right to be here. She had no right to be in his arms, holding him to her, returning his kisses, when it was her fault, and hers alone, that she did not have that right. She had made her decision five years ago. She had chosen a career then, because that was what she thought she wanted, and it was no use now trying to justify her actions by admitting that even she could make a mistake. He might not have married Nicola without coercion, but marry her he had, and she knew, without being told, that he would never break that contract. He still wanted her, that might be true, but she could never hope to share his life with him, or bear his children.

With a supreme effort she dragged herself away from him, putting the straps of her gown in order, tucking wisps of hair back into the coil at her neck. Then, when he stood there regarding her with dark brooding resentment, she put the finishing touches to this ultimate denial.

'I think we must both have drunk too much wine,' she declared, and the faint hysteria in her voice made it sound as if she was amused by what had happened instead of reeling from the pain. 'Honestly, Raf, you can hardly complain about Nicola's behaviour, if you yourself refuse to adhere to the rules!'

CHAPTER NINE

JAIME left the next morning, before Nicola was even awake. Fortunately, she did not see Rafaello again, and she doubted she would have had any breakfast either had the old Contessa not been waiting for her when she came downstairs.

'You are leaving?' she enquired, viewing Jaime's fine wool pants suit without expression. 'I will ask Giulio to fetch down your bags. I imagine you would like a car to take you to the airport.'

Jaime took a deep breath. 'I can phone for a taxi,' she said. 'I assume there are taxis in Vaggio, are there not? Please don't go to any trouble on my account, Contessa. I'd really rather leave with the minimum amount of fuss.'

'I imagine you would,' remarked Rafaello's mother evenly. 'However, I do not believe my son would approve of your trusting yourself to the mercies of Antonio Ponti and his *auto pubblica*, therefore I myself will drive you to Pisa.'

'Oh, really——' Jaime shook her head helplessly, 'I don't think Raf would approve of that either.'

'Happily, I do not have to consider what my son would or would not approve of with regard to myself, Jaime,' the Contessa replied firmly. '*Bene*, you will drink some coffee and eat a croissant while I make the necessary arrangements.'

Jaime had not been driven by the Contessa before,

and for a time, the idiosyncrasies of the old lady's style of motoring kept her thoughts from other things. But gradually, as she began to get used to a staccato kind of rhythm, her mind drifted back to that awful scene with Rafaello.

It was useless trying to pretend he would get over it. Her behaviour must have destroyed any lingering trace of emotion he felt for her. And it was no help telling herself she had done it for his own good. He would never forgive her, and she would never forgive herself for allowing it to happen.

She didn't want to remember the things he had said to her after her outburst. They were such cruel things, such painful things; so much agony and resentment condensed into a vituperative stream of abuse. He had wanted to hurt her, and he had succeeded. He had successfully torn her indifference to shreds, and when he left her in the *salotto* she had felt completely numb.

Unfortunately, the numbness had not lasted. It would have been easier if it had. By the time she had washed and prepared for bed, every jarring nerve in her body was alert to the agony of abandoning all hope, and the tears she had shed had been as much for Raf as for herself. What had she done to him? What had she done to both of them? Could she ever atone for the mistakes of the past?

'Are you leaving because of what Nicola said?'

The Contessa's quiet question brought her abruptly back to an awareness of where she was, and Jaime hastily tried to find excuses for her departure.

'Oh, no,' she exclaimed, smoothing the leather surface of her handbag with nervous fingers. 'I mean, that would be foolish, wouldn't it? After all, it was

Nicola who brought me here.'

'So I believe.' The Contessa's foot pressed a little harder on the accelerator. 'Nevertheless, something must have happened to make you change your mind.'

'Change my mind, Contessa?'

'But of course. If you had had any intention of leaving yesterday, would you not have told me so?'

Jaime sighed. 'It was—I thought it would be the best thing.'

'Best for whom? For you? For Nicola? For my son?'

'For all of us, I suppose,' answered Jaime unwillingly. 'Isn't that a pretty little church?' She pointed to a distant tower. 'Do you know the name of it? I don't remember seeing it before.'

'Talking about churches will not alter the situation, my child. Come, is my son to blame for this sudden flight from Vaggio? You must not allow what he says to upset you. Rafaello has not had an easy life for the past five years, and is it so unnatural that at times he allows his bitterness to show?'

Jaime shook her head. 'I don't blame Rafaello——'

'You blame Nicola?'

'No!' Jaime was vehement. 'I blame myself. If Raf and I had not split up——'

'My child, forgive me, but that is nonsense!'

'Why is it nonsense? Raf believes it.'

'Is that what he said?'

'Among—among other things.'

'Nevertheless, it is nonsense.'

'Why?'

'My dear Jaime, you cannot be blamed for what happened after you and my son separated. Rafaello was not a child; he was—he *is*—an adult. He was not compelled to marry Nicola because you walked out on him.'

'No, but——'

'I know now that Nicola was jealous of you. She has told me so. Oh, not in so many words—she would not be foolish enough to admit to something like that, but her behaviour has left little doubt that she would have done anything in her power to split you two up.'

Jaime bent her head. 'Even so——'

'You cannot deny that the situation might have ended differently if Nicola had not interfered.'

'Who knows?' Jaime lifted her shoulders helplessly. 'I did want my independence—I can't deny that. But whether I would have been strong enough to leave Raf if he hadn't forced me to——'

'*Eccoti*! Who can tell? The dice is cast, and we can only take so much of the responsibility for what may be ordained.'

Jaime glanced towards Rafaello's mother. 'Thank you.'

'Do not thank me.' The Contessa braked with her usual lack of consideration for her passenger. 'I just wonder why Nicola brought you here.'

Jaime hesitated. 'Well, I did try to tell you yesterday.'

The Contessa's lips tightened. 'I wonder now that you should have suggested what you did.'

'Why?' Jaime frowned. 'I promised to try and help Nicola. What else could I do?'

The Contessa took her eyes from the road to gaze at her for so long that eventually Jaime had to guide the steering wheel herself. However, the old lady dragged her eyes away at last, and shaking her head said: 'I do not know what to make of you, *signorina*. Sometimes I think I have been wrong about you, and at others I wonder if I know you at all.'

Jaime felt confused. 'Why should it surprise you that I might want to help Nicola? We were friends.'

'Tell me, *signorina* . . .' the Contessa chose her words with care, 'did you ever love my son?'

Jaime gasped. 'You must know I did!'

'Then in God's name, why do you hate him now?'

'I don't hate him——'

'But you would have him father a child he knows is not his!'

Jaime's jaw dropped. 'What?'

'Oh, do not sound so shocked! You said you knew what was wrong with Nicola. Surely you did not—you *could not* believe that the child was Rafaello's?'

Jaime felt quite faint. It was warm in the car, and although the windows were open, the breeze offered little respite. The collar of her shirt was sticking to the back of her neck, and there was the dampness of moisture along her spine. But now the backs of her knees were sweating, and there were beads of perspiration along her brow; however, what caused the Contessa to bring the car to a halt was the sudden pallor of Jaime's face, and the doubtful suggestion that she was on the point of losing consciousness.

'You did not know?' she demanded, turning to the prostrate girl, and Jaime mutely shook her head. 'But what were you talking about yesterday? I thought you must know about her and Lorenzo. What else could you think would cause me such distress?'

Jaime's mouth felt parched, but after a few minutes she managed to speak. 'I thought—I thought you were talking about Nicola drinking,' she confessed. 'I didn't know—I never connected her—her morning sickness with—with a baby.'

'Then you are extremely naïve,' remarked the Contessa drily. 'Or——' she shrugged her shoulders in a typically continental gesture, 'your own feelings of guilt have blinded you to anyone else's.'

Jaime gulped. 'I'm so sorry.'

'Yes, so am I.' The Contessa expelled her breath wearily.

'So—so that was what you meant when you said Raf knew, that everybody knew?'

'Of course.'

'Nicola and—and Lorenzo?'

'Rafaello's half-brother,' declared the Contessa bitterly. 'My husband got one of the kitchen staff with child.'

Jaime gasped. 'So that's why Lorenzo is so—so——'

'Arrogant? But yes. Can you imagine how I felt the day I arrived to find you and he together?'

Jaime caught her lip between her teeth. 'You had no need to feel concerned on my account, Contessa. I've worked with men like Lorenzo Costa. That's one of the advantages of having a career—one learns to be wary of a certain type of man.'

'Men like my husband,' declared the Contessa flatly. 'Oh, I loved Ricardo dearly, but I was not blind to his faults. Nicola, I regret to say, does not learn by her mistakes.'

Jaime rubbed her damp palms down over her knees. 'I just don't understand what she wanted of me.'

'Nor do I, now you tell me you do not know the truth,' mused the Contessa thoughtfully. 'Unless she thought you might help her to find a way to lose the child, as she did before.'

Jaime blinked. 'Surely it wasn't Nicola's fault that the baby she had was born dead?'

'That, no. But losing it—oh, yes, I am afraid Nicola was to blame for that.' She sighed. 'I expect Rafaello told you about it. It was a terrible affair.'

'As—as a matter of fact, Raf didn't tell me,' Jaime admitted uncomfortably. 'It was Lorenzo, the morning after I arrived. He told me there had been a child that died.'

'He would!' muttered the Contessa vehemently. 'He has always been jealous of Rafaello, even though my son has supported him for years.' Her lips curled. 'And what did he tell you about it? Did he cast doubt about the child's parentage? He would not be the first to do so.'

Jaime's colour returned slowly, but she still had that peculiar sense of unreality, that feeling of a situation totally beyond her comprehension. No wonder Rafaello was so bitter, she thought with dismay. No wonder there was so much bitterness between them. Nicola had brought her here under false pretences, and although her heart ached for Rafaello, Jaime knew she had no choice but to leave.

The Contessa did not accompany her into the airport itself. They said their goodbyes outside—two women who might have been related, separated by a gulf neither one of them could breach.

'I will tell Rafaello the truth,' his mother promised, after Jaime had climbed out of the car. 'Not that you love him. I am too good a Catholic for that, and I do not know what he might do if he believed it. But I will

tell him you did not know of Nicola's condition.
Perhaps that may give him some consolation.'

Jaime was trembling as the old Mercedes drove
away. In a few words, the Contessa had exposed the
deepest secret of her heart, and left her vulnerable . . .

It was late in the evening when Jaime got back to her
apartment, and she half expected Mrs Purdom to be
out. But that lady was watching television in her
sitting room when she heard Jaime's key in the lock,
and her greeting was warmly reassuring as she helped
her mistress off with her jacket.

London, predictably enough, was suffering the
effects of a seasonal downpour, and it was a relief to
get into the apartment, where an efficient central
heating system soon dispelled the chilling dampness of
the evening.

'I must say, you've chosen the wrong night to come
home,' the housekeeper tutted, shaking the moisture
from Jaime's jacket, which had accumulated in the
short dash from the taxi. 'And you don't look
particularly rested either. Are you sure you haven't
been camping out at the office?'

Jaime forced a polite chuckle, but her heart was not
in it, and as if gleaning this, Mrs Purdom gave up her
attempt to be facetious. 'I'm sure what you need is a
good hot meal,' she declared, carrying Jaime's suitcase
into her bedroom. 'You take off these wet clothes and
relax for a while, and I'll soon have something ready
for you.'

'Oh, really, Mrs Purdom——' Jaime found it
difficult to find the right words without sounding
ungrateful. 'I'm not particularly hungry, honestly.

A—a sandwich, perhaps, and a cup of tea. I don't think I could eat anything else.'

'Hmm! Well——' Mrs Purdom arched her brows in some disdain, 'if that's what you want.'

'It is.' Jaime sank down on to the side of her bed wearily. 'In about three-quarters of an hour. I'm going to take a bath first.'

Relaxing in the scented water, Jaime tried to empty her mind of thoughts of Rafaello and Nicola and the old Contessa, but it was impossible. Already she was wondering what both Rafaello and Nicola had made of her hasty departure, and while she guessed Rafaello would be glad she had gone, about Nicola she was not so sure. She hoped the other girl would not do anything foolish now she was no longer there to dissuade her, but if Nicola's bid to divert attention had rebounded on her, she had only herself to blame. Surely she could not really believe that Rafaello was in ignorance of her condition? And what had possessed her to get involved with Lorenzo Costa? Jaime couldn't believe it was her desire for a baby that had driven her into the other man's arms.

The enigma still remained as to why Nicola had invited *her* to Italy. What could she have possibly hoped Jaime would achieve? Her pleas for Jaime to intercede on her behalf had a hollow ring now, and as she had not been completely honest about that, why should Jaime believe anything she said?

It was strange to climb into her own bed later, but infinitely reassuring to anticipate the resumption of her normal life. It would be quite a relief to get back to the office. The usual abrasive relationship she had with her contemporaries was exactly what she needed to shake off the sense of depression that was gripping her, and she forced herself to think of the new promotion and its implications for her career.

Martin Longman poured more champagne into Jaime's glass and raised his own towards her. 'A great success, wouldn't you say?' he declared, with obvious satisfaction. 'I think my fellow directors are going to be pleased. Lady-Free is going to break all records.'

'Do you think so?'

Jaime sipped her champagne thoughtfully, and her boss regarded her with troubled eyes. 'Don't you? Don't you feel we've got a winner on our hands? Jaime, it's all down to you. Don't get cold feet now.'

'Oh, I'm not.' Jaime forced a faint smile to her lips. 'I just don't like—anticipating success, that's all. Hmm, this is delicious, but I really think I've had enough.'

'It's nothing to do with the launch, is it?' Martin put down his own glass and regarded her solemnly. 'You've not been yourself since you came back from Italy. What is it, Jaime? What's wrong? I thought you said your friend had recovered. You're not still worrying about her, are you?'

'Worrying about Nicola?' Jaime's voice lifted an octave. 'No. No, I'm not worrying about anything.'

'But something's wrong, Jaime—I know it.' Martin came round his desk to prop his hips against the corner. 'You don't have the same enthusiasm you used to. I'm not saying your work is suffering—you're too conscientious for that. But, quite frankly, you're beginning to worry me. It's obvious you've lost weight, and I want to know why.'

'Oh, don't be silly, Martin.' Jaime buried her nose in the slim glass she was holding. 'I've been on a diet, that's all. All that Italian food, it's awfully bad for the figure.'

'Jaime, stop it!' Martin's fair features were flushed with impatience. 'I know you too well. Good heavens, we've worked together for almost a year. I thought we were friends.'

'We are. And it's sweet of you to worry about me, honestly, but——' She looked up at him hopefully, and then, recognising the stubbornness of his expression, she sighed. 'It's a personal matter, Martin, something I have to work out myself. There's nothing I can do about it. I just have to give it time. Really, I'm not about to desert the company.'

'Thank goodness for that!' Martin was fervent. 'And you don't want to talk about it?' You don't think another opinion might help?'

Jaime shook her head. 'I don't think so.'

'It's a man, obviously.' He paused. 'Someone you met in Italy?'

Jaime hesitated. 'You might say that,' she conceded, putting down her glass. 'Do you mind if I go now, Martin? I do have the beginnings of a headache.'

'And I was going to ask you to join me for dinner,' said Martin wryly. 'I don't suppose you . . .'

'I'd rather not. Not tonight,' replied Jaime apologetically. 'An early night is in order. I've used so much nervous energy today, I need to recharge my batteries.'

'I wish I believed that was all it was,' commented Martin flatly. 'It's nearly two weeks, Jaime. How much longer is it going to take?'

'I wish I knew.' Jaime tried to make light of it. 'I'll see you on Monday, Martin. And—thanks. For everything.'

Martin Longman was not the only person who was worried about Jaime. Mrs Purdom was too, and Jaime knew her housekeeper expended a lot of energy at mealtimes, trying to tempt her with some new delicacy. Lately, there had been fragrant broths and light soufflés, fluffy eggs that melted on the tongue; there had been tender green vegetables, served with mouthwatering sauces, and crisply-flaky *vol-au-vents*, oozing with ham or cheese or chicken. Jaime felt obliged to at least try everything that was put before her, which she guessed was Mrs Purdom's intention, but her appetite had dwindled and she found it almost impossible to make the effort. Martin was right, she had lost her enthusiasm—for everything—and her life which had once seemed so full now seemed frighteningly empty.

This evening Mrs Purdom had some rather disturbing news to impart, however. There had been a call for her, from Italy: 'That woman who rang before,' she admitted with some reluctance. Like Martin Longman, the housekeeper could only attribute Jaime's unhappiness to something that had happened in Italy, and she was loath to revive a memory that was evidently painful to her. 'I told her I didn't know when you'd be back.'

Jaime kicked off her shoes and walked into her living room. 'Why did you tell her that, Mrs Purdom?' she asked, her thoughts already racing at this long-delayed development. She had expected Nicola to ring two weeks ago. Why had she waited so long?

'I didn't know whether you'd want to speak to her, Miss Forster,' the housekeeper replied stiffly, aware of the rebuke. 'I—she said she would ring again tomorrow. I assumed that was for the best.'

Jaime sank down on to the couch, loosening her hair, and as she did so, her impatience at Mrs Purdom's behaviour evaporated. 'You're probably right,' she conceded, her smile relieving the housekeeper's taut expression. 'I am rather tired this evening, and Signora di Vaggio can be rather—demanding.'

'That's what I thought,' said Mrs Purdom, recovering her composure. 'Now, I've got a nice piece of fish for you this evening. Would you prefer asparagus tips or broccoli?'

With the irrelevant question of which vegetable to choose behind her, Jaime slumped back wearily against the cushions. Nicola had rung! After two weeks of wondering what was going on, she had finally chosen to enlighten her, and although Jaime did not look forward to her call, she knew it was inevitable. Sooner or later she had to speak to Nicola, and perhaps, with that burden behind her, she could shake off this feeling of despair and misery.

The phone rang again as Jaime was having dinner. Even though Mrs Purdom had said Nicola had promised to ring back the next day, Jaime sensed who was calling, and it was no surprise when the housekeeper confirmed her suspicions.

'Do you want to speak to her now?' she asked, her hand over the mouthpiece, and although Jaime was tempted to decline, she nodded her head.

'I might as well,' she said, getting up from her chair. 'Thank you, Mrs Purdom.'

Jaime waited until the housekeeper had left the room and then took a calming breath. 'Hello, Nicola,' she said, unable to keep her tone as expressionless as she could have wished. 'What a surprise! I wasn't expecting you to ring.'

'Weren't you?' Nicola sounded amazingly casual. 'I was sure you would be.'

'Two weeks ago, yes,' conceded Jaime shortly, 'I did anticipate some reaction to my departure. But now . . .'

'Well, you know how it is.' Nicola was indifferent. 'I was pretty mad at you, really—running out on me like that.'

Jaime steeled herself. 'I didn't exactly run out on you, Nicola. Your mother-in-law knew where I'd gone. I—thought it was the only thing to do.'

'Did you?' Nicola paused. 'I didn't realise you'd be so sensitive, Jaime.'

'What do you mean?'

Nicola made a careless sound. 'Well, taking offence at what I said, of course. I assume that was why you felt the need to make your point.'

Jaime sighed. 'You lied to me, Nicola. You brought me out to Vaggio on a totally dishonest pretext. You said you were desperate to have a child. You omitted to say that you were already carrying one!'

'I thought you guessed.' To Jaime's amazement, Nicola did not sound perturbed. 'That morning I was sick, I thought you knew.'

'How could I?'

'I thought you were experienced, Jaime. I thought

you were a woman of the world.'

'You forget——' Jaime paused a moment, calming her outburst. 'You forget, you told me you wanted me to plead with Raf on your behalf!'

Nicola sighed. 'Oh—well, yes, I did say that, didn't I? And to a certain extent it was true. But I knew if I told you the truth before you left England, you never would have come.'

'You can bet on it!'

'You sound vehement, Jaime——'

'I am. How could you, Nicola? How could you? You wanted me to intercede on your behalf for another man's child!'

'I suppose my dear mother-in-law told you that,' Nicola sniffed. 'Now you can understand why I didn't want the old witch to come here. I knew she'd try to poison your mind against me.'

Jaime was astounded. 'Nicola, you can't honestly expect Raf's mother to condone what you've done!'

'Why not? Lorenzo's her husband's son, just as much as Raf is.'

Jaime felt sick. 'So you did know!'

'Of course. It's common knowledge. Ever since Raf took him on as chauffeur, he's made no secret of it.'

'Oh, Nicola——'

'Don't be such a prig, Jaime. Your life hasn't been so blameless you can criticise me for making one mistake.'

'*One mistake!*'

'All right, two, then,' exclaimed Nicola incredibly. 'I suppose that old woman told you about Antonio Ponti. Well, the child wasn't his, no matter what she says.'

Jaime swallowed convulsively. So this was what the Contessa had hinted at. There had been another man, before Lorenzo Costa. And that relationship had ended in tragedy, with the death of Rafaello's son.

'Well?' Nicola didn't like Jaime's silence, and was quick to justify herself. 'I couldn't help it that I lost the baby, could I? The roads around here are dangerous—I've told Raf so, a hundred times. If we'd been living in Rome, as I wanted, I wouldn't have lost the child. But Antonio was driving too fast, and——'

Jaime put a trembling hand to her throat. 'But *why*, Nicola? Why?'

'Why what? Why did I lose the child? I should have thought that was obvious. We crashed——'

'I mean, why did you do it? You married Raf, Nicola! You wanted to marry him. For heaven's sake, what went wrong?'

Nicola sniffed again. 'I told you—I hate it here. I hate it! There's no fun; there's nothing to do——'

'But you knew that before you married Raf.'

'How could I? He was different in London. He seemed dangerous, and exciting; and I was bored!'

Jaime shook her head. She didn't want to hear any more. It was all so much worse than she had imagined, and remembering the way she had accused Rafaello of causing the servants to lose respect for her, she felt bitterly ashamed.

'Anyway,' went on Nicola carelessly, 'you can't talk. You didn't stay here very long, did you? You soon made an excuse to leave.'

'I didn't *make* an excuse, Nicola——'

'Okay, so you left anyway. The fact remains, you

wouldn't want to be locked up in a castle for the rest of your life!'

Jaime moistened her lips. If only she had the chance, she thought despairingly. She knew she would give everything she possessed to have the chance to start again.

'So,' Nicola accepted her silence as answer enough, 'you'll be pleased to hear that your visit did some good, after all.'

'Some good?' Jaime felt numb.

'Yes.' Nicola hesitated. 'Raf's finally agreed that I can live at the apartment in Rome. It's a sort of compromise, really. He knows he can't divorce me, but he doesn't want me to have the baby at Vaggio. So he's letting me live at the apartment, at least until after the baby is due, and it will give us both a chance to get things into perspective.'

'I see.'

'It's all thanks to you,' went on Nicola comfortably. 'I mean, I thought he was going to throw me out, and to hell with his religion. But you must have said something that struck a responsive chord. This morning he told me his decision, and as you can imagine, I was delighted. I'm leaving at the end of the week, and I just wanted you to know that I'm grateful!'

CHAPTER TEN

'MISS FORSTER, there's been a telephone call for you.'

'Oh, damn!' Jaime looked up from the balance sheets she had been studying with uncharacteristic impatience. She had spent the morning closeted with the designer Martin had chosen to produce plans for the proposed new fashion line, and since they had not been able to agree, she was in no mood to be distracted now. 'Look, whoever calls, tell them I'll get back to them, Diane,' she declared, pushing the spectacles she had been forced to acquire two months before up her nose. 'I've got to get these finished by five o'clock, and I want to leave early because of that dinner at the Dorchester.'

'It was your housekeeper, actually, Miss Forster,' said Diane purposefully, unwilling to take her dismissal. 'I told her you were busy, but she insisted I give you the message.'

'What message?' Jaime lifted her head again, an unpleasant feeling of coldness gripping the pit of her stomach. It had taken six months for her to at last stop quaking every time her home telephone rang, but now, hearing that it was Mrs Purdom on the other end of the line, she was experiencing that familiar sense of panic. It couldn't be Nicola, she told herself severely, not after all this time. But the feeling persisted, all the same.

'She said to tell you, you had a visitor, Miss

Forster,' Diane explained smoothly. 'A-a Signora di Vaggio. Would that be the same Signora di Vaggio who rang you before?'

It was Nicola! Jaime's mouth dried up, causing an awful constricted feeling in her throat. Heavens, what did Nicola want now? Surely she must have had the baby. What earthly reason could she have for going to the apartment unannounced? She must have known Jaime would be at work, so why hadn't she contacted her there?

Aware that Diane was waiting for some response, Jaime cleared her throat. 'Oh—I—yes. Yes, I expect it is,' she murmured, wondering if she looked as shaken as she felt. 'Did—er—did Mrs Purdom say anything else?'

'Only that she thought you would like to know about the lady, Miss Forster. I suppose she expects you to go home and see her.'

Jaime chewed helplessly at her lower lip. 'Yes,' she said, absently, 'yes, perhaps she does.' Then she sighed. 'Oh, blast! What am I going to do?'

'Well, I could finish checking those sheets for you, Miss Forster,' Diane offered tentatively. 'And you do have at least three hours before you need start for the dinner.'

Jaime expelled her breath on a sound half of hysteria. Of course, Diane assumed she was worried about her business appointments. Fortunately, she hadn't associated Jaime's plea for assistance from a higher authority with her unexpected visitor.

'You're right,' Jaime said now, coming to a decision. 'There's nothing so desperately urgent that it can't wait another day. Don't worry about the balance sheets, Diane. I'll get back to them tomorrow. Just get me Mr Longman on the phone, would you? I must keep him informed of what I'm doing.'

'Yes, Miss Forster.'

Diane went away, and presently the intercom buzzed to announce that she had Martin Longman for her. 'Putting you through,' she said, pressing switches, and presently Martin's deeper tones proclaimed his presence at the other end of the line.

'Did you have a problem?' he asked goodhumouredly, and Jaime was glad she had not caught him on a bad day. 'I hear from Steve Berlitz that you weren't too enamoured of his drawings. I think perhaps you were a little hasty. I rather like the image he was creating.'

Jaime sighed. 'If what you're wanting to promote is that little-girl look, then go ahead,' she declared tautly. 'It's popular enough, I guess, with the teenage element among our consumers.'

'I see.' Martin acknowledged the rebuke with a wry tone. 'You're saying that our consumers are a little older than that?'

'We aim to reach the twenty to thirty age group, Martin, you know that. And quite honestly, I can't see our clients dressed in baggy dungarees and frilly miniskirts.'

'Point taken.' Martin expelled his breath resignedly. 'So we aim for something a little more sophisticated, but is Berlitz the chap to do it?'

'I honestly don't know, Martin.' Jaime tried to keep the impatience out of her voice. 'But right now, that's not my problem.' She paused. 'As a matter of fact, something unexpected has come up—at home. I'm ringing to ask whether you have any objections if I leave right away.'

'Nothing serious, I hope.' Martin sounded concerned now. 'Your housekeeper hasn't had an accident, has she? It's so easy to do something silly——'

'It's not Mrs Purdom,' said Jaime firmly. 'I—— a friend—— a friend has turned up unexpectedly. I think I ought to go and see what she wants.'

Martin hesitated. 'It wouldn't be this—— friend—— from Italy again?'

'What makes you ask that?'

'You do, Jaime, you do. It's not like you to go rushing off at a moment's notice. And I can't think of anyone else, except your mother, who might turn up unexpectedly.'

'I don't think my mother is likely to do that,' remarked Jaime tensely, tapping her pen on the blotting pad in front of her. 'And—— yes, as it happens, it is Signora di Vaggio. I'm sorry, Martin. I know this is a busy time——'

'Nonsense!' Martin dismissed her apologies. 'There's nothing spoiling here. Just don't forget about that dinner this evening. I'm depending on you to represent the company.'

'I won't forget.' Jaime was relieved. 'Thanks, Martin. I'll see you tomorrow.'

'Yes.' Martin paused. 'You know, we should open an office in Italy. That way you'd be on hand every time this friend of yours gets into difficulties!'

It was a cold afternoon, and when Jaime left the office, lights were already springing up all over the city. It would soon be Christmas, and the shops were strung with coloured lights, but Jaime was too wrapped up in her own problems to pay much attention to their gay displays.

Mrs Purdom met her in the hall of the apartment, her homely face flushed and anxious. 'I'm sorry I had to ring you at the office, Miss Forster,' she exclaimed, helping Jaime off with her jacket and taking her briefcase. 'But really, when Signora di Vaggio turned up, I——'

'That's all right, Mrs Purdom.' Jaime mentally steeled herself to face the newcomer. 'Is—is the *signora* alone? I mean, she hasn't brought anyone with her? Not—not a baby, or anything?'

'A baby?' Mrs Purdom frowned. 'Oh, no, Miss Forster, she's quite alone. And—and rather tired, if you don't mind me saying so. It's probably been quite a journey for a woman of her age.'

'*Of her age!*' Jaime blinked, and passing Mrs Purdom, she quickly thrust open the door of her living room. As she had half suspected, the old Contessa was seated in the armchair beneath the branching standard lamp, and at Jaime's appearance she came immediately to her feet.

'Good afternoon, *signorina*,' she greeted her formally. 'I hope you will forgive this intrusion. But I wanted to speak to you and I could not entrust what I have to say to the telephone.'

'*Contessa!*' The word fell from Jaime's lips, and hearing it, Mrs Purdom caught her breath behind her.

'I didn't know——' she began, clicking her tongue, and then was silenced by the imperious old lady from across the room.

'Please assure your housekeeper that I am not offended, *signorina*,' she declared, addressing herself to Jaime. 'I seldom use a title when I am travelling abroad. It is of no value, a courtesy thing, no more. I am happy to be Signora di Vaggio, and if she would be so kind I should like the tea now she offered me earlier.'

Jaime looked at Mrs Purdom and the housekeeper lifted her shoulders in a helpless gesture. 'Tea for two,' she said, with a wry grimace, and Jaime closed the door behind her as the woman went away.

'You are surprised to see me, *signorina*.' It was a statement, not a question. 'But the good—— Mrs Purdom, is it? *Si*, she telephoned you with the news, did she not?'

Jaime took a deep breath. 'She said I had a visitor,' she murmured weakly. 'I'm sorry. Do sit down again. I'm sure I must look as foolish as I feel.'

'Foolish? Why should you feel foolish?' The Contessa subsided again, with evident relief. 'Perhaps you were expecting someone else, no? Perhaps my arrival is a disappointment.'

'Oh, no.' Jaime shook her head and moved rather unsteadily away from the door. 'On the contrary, I'm delighted to see you, *contessa*. I thought—oh, it doesn't matter what I thought. How are you? Are you well? What are you doing in London?'

The Contessa regarded her thoughtfully for a moment, and then, when Jaime was beginning to feel uncomfortable, she said: 'You have lost weight, *signorina*. You are working too hard.'

'Probably.' Jaime was grateful for the respite to recover her composure, and managed a faint smile.

'I'm hoping to take a holiday once Christmas is over. It's been rather hectic since the holiday season began.'

'You work for a—cosmetics company, do you not?' the old lady queried, straightening a pleat in her skirt. 'This work—it means a lot to you, does it not? You have never regretted your decision to choose a career.'

Jaime worked her way round the couch and sank down on to its soft cushions. 'Well, almost never,' she conceded, with a forced attempt at humour. 'But never mind about me, what are you doing in England? Are you on your way to America?'

'Now why should you think that?' asked the Contessa, arching her thin aristocratic brows.

'Well, I remember——' Jaime paused, and then went on reluctantly: 'The Christmas Raf spent in England, he—he told me you were visiting some member of your family in San Francisco.'

'Ah, yes,' the old lady nodded. 'I went to see my brother Enzo that year. His wife had just died. That was why I was away from my own family.' She hesitated. 'Otherwise, Rafaello would not have spent Christmas in England.'

Jaime looked down at her linked fingers. 'I suppose not.'

'Tell me,' the Contessa spoke urgently, 'have you heard from Rafaello recently?'

'Heard from Raf——' Jaime looked across at her, startled. 'Why, no. No, of course not. Wh-why should you think I might?'

The return of Mrs Purdom with the tea tray briefly interrupted their conversation, and while the house-keeper placed the tray on a low table within reach of her mistress, Jaime tried to make sense of what the

Contessa was asking. Why should Rafaello's mother suspect that her son might have been in touch with her? Had he and Nicola split up? And if they had, why would the Contessa come to her, knowing as she did how Jaime felt about Raphael?

The housekeeper assured herself that they had everything they needed, and then withdrew, leaving Jaime to pour the tea. Her hand shook as she lifted the teapot, but her voice was tolerably steady as she asked the Contessa whether she preferred milk or lemon.

'Oh, milk, please. And a little sugar,' replied the old lady firmly. 'An aunt of my father's introduced me to the English way of taking tea, and I have never had the inclination to try it any other.'

There were tiny salmon and cucumber sandwiches, and some of Mrs Purdom's fruit scones, but neither of the women seemed particularly hungry. Rafaello's mother nibbled on a slice of rich madeira cake, but Jaime eschewed everything, waiting with some impatience for the Contessa to explain herself.

'So—Rafaello has not written to you or telephoned you?' the old lady asked at last, cradling her cup between her fingers.

'No.' Jaime was abrupt. 'You must know he hasn't. If—if that's why you've come here, then I'm afraid you've had a wasted journey.'

The Contessa sighed. 'Forgive me, I am explaining myself badly.' She hesitated. 'Asking you these questions, Jaime—please, do not regard them as a criticism; rather as a final justification.'

'A justification?' Jaime was bewildered. 'A justification for what?'

'For coming here. For bringing you some news,

which you may or may not wish to hear.'

'What news?' Jaime put down her cup and pressed her hands together. 'I-I suppose Nicola has had the baby. Is that what you came to tell me? Well, why should you think Raf might have bothered to let me know?'

The Contessa put down her cup, too, and regarded the girl sitting opposite her with troubled eyes. 'You do not know?' she exclaimed. 'You have not heard?'

'Heard? Heard what?' Jaime was beside herself. '*Contessa*, I have heard nothing since Nicola rang me to tell me she was moving to the apartment in Rome.'

'Oh——' The Contessa cupped her cheek with an astonished hand. 'But I thought—I assumed—the Temples are friends of yours, are they not?'

'The Temples? Oh, you mean Nicola's parents. Well—no, not exactly. Nicola and I met at school. I hardly know her parents.'

'So they did not inform you that Nicola—died?'

Jaime's shoulders sagged. 'Nicola—*died*?' she echoed faintly. 'No. No, no one told me anything. Oh *God*! I had no idea.'

The Contessa nodded. 'I did wonder, but then——' She spread her hands, 'I was sure you would hear.'

'No. No, nothing.' Jaime could feel a faint throbbing starting in her temple as she spoke. 'When—when did it happen?'

The old lady folded her hands. 'The funeral was some six weeks ago.'

'Six weeks!'

'*Si*. She was buried in the family vault at Vaggio.'

'Six weeks!' Jaime couldn't get over it. Then, trying to gather her thoughts, she added: 'The baby! Had she had the baby? Was it a boy or a girl?'

'A girl,' the Contessa replied quietly. 'It lived only minutes after it was delivered.'

'Oh! Oh, poor Nicola!' Jaime could find it in her heart to pity the girl. 'She must have been shattered!'

'She did not know,' said the Contessa gently. 'She died before the Caesarian operation was carried out—something to do with that miscarriage she had. There was nothing anyone could do.'

'Oh, *God*!' Jaime put her head in her hands. 'Poor Nicola!'

'It was—tragic,' agreed the Contessa heavily. 'Rafaello was with her when she died. He felt somehow responsible, even though he knew Lorenzo had visited her since she went to live at the apartment.'

'Was—was Lorenzo there, too?'

'When she died? Oh, no. Lorenzo has found himself a new protector, an American widow, who has more money than brains. She has taken him to the United States. They left several weeks before the child was born.'

'But—it was *his* child!'

The Contessa shrugged. 'He had no intention of claiming it as such. He knew that so long as Rafaello and Nicola were married, the child would be accepted as theirs. He knew Rafaello would not allow the child to suffer for its parents' infidelities.'

Jaime made a helpless gesture. 'He—he's completely amoral!'

'Perhaps.' the Contessa inclined her head. 'Myself, I am glad he is out of my son's life. Whatever happens, that is a blessing.'

Jaime gestured towards the tray, but when the Contessa declined any further refreshment, she said: 'Well, thank you, for letting me know about—about Nicola. I am grateful——'

'Wait!' The Contessa held up her hand. 'That is not why I came.'

'It's not?' Jaime was confused. 'But I thought——'

'Jaime, I told you: I thought you knew. My reasons for coming here have to do with Rafaello, not Nicola. I thought I had made that clear.'

Jaime licked her lips. 'No. No, you didn't. I-I'm sorry, but I assumed you wanted to find out whether Raf had told me.'

'I did. But that was not why I came.' The Contessa paused. 'Jaime, if I ask you a very personal question, will you give me an honest answer?'

'If I can.' Jaime shifted back into the cushions, her voice a little unsteady. 'But—but if you're going to tell me to keep out of Raf's life, then don't bother. I-I have no intention of opening up old wounds.'

'You have not?' Rafaello's mother gazed at her with some dismay, and Jaime shook her head.

'No. No, you needn't worry, *contessa*, I realise how you must feel. If—if things had been different—well, who knows how I'd have answered, but now I can see you would want to assure yourself that Raf doesn't make the same mistakes again.'

'No, you are wrong!' burst out the old lady fiercely. 'Jaime, you have misunderstood me completely. I did not come here to tell you to keep out of my son's life; quite the reverse. He needs you, Jaime. He needs you desperately. But as proud as he is, he will never tell you so himself!'

Jaime stared at her. 'What do you mean?'

'What do you think I mean, Jaime? You made your choice very plain all those years ago. Do you think I could ever convince him that you had had second thoughts?'

Jaime swallowed convulsively. 'You—you know, don't you?'

'That you still love my son?' The Contessa nodded. 'Oh, yes, I know that. From the moment we met, I knew it. But do you love him enough to sacrifice your career for his sake? That is something I do not know.'

Jaime got up from the couch and walked nervously across the room. Then, turning, she looked down at the old lady. 'When—when I first met Raf, I was eighteen. As—as I told you, my father had walked out on my mother when I was just a child. If it hadn't been for a cousin of my mother's, I should never have had the kind of education I had. But I did, and—and I suppose I felt I owed it to myself to do something with it.'

'And Rafaello?'

'Raf?' Jaime hesitated. 'Oh—Raf was something else. He was all the things my mother had taught me to avoid. A man who was handsome, who was attractive to women! A man who could take all my carefully drawn plans of making a career for myself, and screw them up.'

'Yet you let him go.'

'Yes.' Jaime bent her head. 'Yes, I did that. And regretted it immediately afterwards.'

'No——'

'Oh, yes.' Jaime's lips twisted. 'But can you imagine how I felt when I discovered he was going to marry

Nicola? The announcement was made less than a month after—after—— Well! It was enough to convince me that my doubts had been justified.'

'Oh, Jaime!'

'So now you see, it isn't really a question of my feelings at all. It's Raf's. He—he despises me. He's still physically attracted to me, but he doesn't love me. I don't know how you could think he did.'

'Jaime, all I know is that since we buried Nicola, my son has been like—like a dead man.' The Contessa shook her head. 'I tried to tell myself it was because of Nicola, and in the beginning I almost convinced myself, but it is not so. I realise now that this is not some new condition. Maria tells me he has not eaten a good meal in months, and I am afraid he is working himself to death.'

Jaime caught her breath. 'And—and you think I can change that?'

'I hope and pray you can. Jaime, Rafaello loved you, I know that. Whether he still does is something you must find out. But he will never come to you, so I am appealing to you to go to him.'

Martin took the news that Jaime was going to Italy philosophically. 'I can't say it's entirely unexpected,' he commented, from behind his square mahogany desk. 'Much as I hate to say it, you haven't been yourself since you came back, and it will do you good to get this thing out of your system, once and for all.'

'And if I don't?' murmured Jaime unhappily. 'Get it out of my system, I mean.'

'Then I suppose I'll have to think seriously about that Italian branch,' replied Martin casually, and

Jaime leant across and kissed him for his understanding.

Getting a flight to Pisa wasn't difficult. At this time of year, most people were planning a Christmas break, and as it was still ten days to the festivities, Jaime had no problems.

In Pisa, she hired a car to take her the final miles of her journey. In truth, she was not enthusiastic about driving about these country roads in icy conditions, but it was the quickest way she could think of getting there. And she wanted to get there. She wanted to see Rafaello's face when she turned up. She wanted to hear his voice when he spoke to her. She wanted to find out once and for all exactly what they had, or whether time, and misunderstandings, had destroyed that elusive desire. Passion was not love; sex was not love; but if that was all he could offer, would it be enough?

It was early evening when she drove up the final twisting track to the castle. Darkness had fallen some time before, and on the dark unfamiliar roads, Jaime had found it difficult to find her way. She half wished she had asked the Contessa to come with her, but that lady had insisted Jaime came alone.

'Rafaello must not know I came to you,' she said, in some agitation. 'He would never forgive me. Promise me you will not tell him. I do not know what he would do if he knew.'

The Castello yard was dark and deserted, and indeed, if Jaime had not had the Contessa's word that Rafaello was at the Castello, she would have had doubts. There seemed to be no lights anywhere, but the curtains were drawn, and their heavy folds disguised any illumination within.

Knocking at the studded door, Jaime wondered if anyone would hear her. The iron bell-pull was merely ornamental, and no one had installed anything incongruous like an electric system. Allowing the heavy brass ring to fall against the solid wood once more, Jaime had half decided to seek accommodation in Vaggio for the night and return to the Castello in the morning, when the door finally swung inward.

'Signorina Forster!'

It was the housekeeper, Maria, who had answered her summons, and she stared at Jaime in dismay. For one awful moment Jaime wondered if some other tragedy had occurred of which she was in ignorance, but evidently Maria's distress was not what she feared.

'Oh, *la signora* is not here, *signorina*,' she exclaimed, her hands fluttering nervously to her full bosom. 'Signorina Forster, you have had a—how do you say?—a journey for nothing! *La signora—la signora è morta!*'

'I know, Maria.' Jaime wished she would invite her in. It was a bitterly cold evening, and she had left her overcoat in the car. Standing here, waiting for someone to answer the door, she had got chilled to the bone, and she looked with some longing at the fire burning in the hall grate behind the housekeeper. 'I didn't——'

'*Chi è*, Maria?'

The weary masculine tones caused her to break off abruptly, and as she stood there shivering in the wind, Rafaello appeared from the direction of the library. He was pushing back his hair as he spoke, his head inclined slightly forward, so that he didn't immediately recognise the visitor. But then, as Maria turned to him, spreading her hands bewilderedly, he lifted his head, and Jaime paled at the sudden bleakness of his expression.

'*La signorina è qui, signore,*' Maria explained, with a lingering trace of doubt in her voice. 'I-I have told her—*la signora* is dead!'

'I knew,' exclaimed Jaime, realising she would have to take the initiative before he ordered her to leave. Brushing past the startled housekeeper, she entered the hall of the castle, holding out her hands to the fire's warmth and adding: 'Will you ask Giulio to bring in my bags? It's so cold, and I've been waiting for ages for someone to hear me.'

Rafaello looked as though he might refuse, but then, as if aware that Maria was watching him and that she expected a certain code of conduct from him, he nodded. '*Il bagaglio*, Maria, *per favore*,' he directed tersely, and to Jaime: 'You had better come into the library.'

There was a fire in the library, too, casting its warmth over the shelves of books, adding a certain intimacy to its austere interior. Rafaello had evidently been working at the desk, and a lamp was lit to give him light, illuminating the columns of figures he had been studying, the gold fountain pen, which had been thrown down when he went to investigate the interruption.

'Sit down,' he essayed shortly, closing the door behind them and walking towards his desk. 'Do you want a drink? I have some cognac, if you are really cold.'

'Thank you.'

Jaime sank into one of the leather armchairs, watching him as he approached the cabinet, watching his hands as he handled the decanter and glasses. She thought the decanter rattled as it struck the glass, but she couldn't be absolutely certain. What she was certain was that his mother had not been exaggerating. Rafaello had lost some weight; the suede trousers and matching waistcoat hung on his disturbingly thin frame.

When he turned to hand her the glass, she had a proper chance to look at his face, and what she saw there filled her with alarm. Surely Rafaello was ill, or suffering from some wasting disease, she thought. She had never seen a man's face change so much, or witnessed so much condemnation in one freezing glance.

'Thank you,' she said now, taking the glass from him jerkily, and immediately averting her eyes. This was going to be so much harder than she had imagined, and already she was half prepared to believe that the Contessa had been wrong. Rafaello did not want her. His grief was not consequent on her behaviour. She had been a fool to come here on an old woman's whim, when Rafaello evidently saw no merit in her unwelcome intrusion.

She was not given long to compose her arguments. 'Why have you come?' he demanded, propping himself against the side of the desk and regarding her with cold inimical eyes. 'I suppose it was unreasonable to hope that you might not find out that my wife was dead. I imagine you have come here to offer me your belated condolences.' His lips twisted. 'There was no need. If you felt you had to acknowledge the event, a letter would have sufficed.'

Jaime took a determined sip of the brandy, then, wincing at its raw strength, she forced herself to speak. 'How cold you are, Raf,' she murmured, evading a direct answer. 'I was—sorry to hear of Nicola's death, but that wasn't why I came.'

'It was not?' There was no glimmer of interest in his voice. 'I cannot conceive of any other reason you might have to make this journey in winter.'

'Can't you, Raf? Can't you?' Jaime steeled herself to face that contemptuous stare. 'I really don't believe that. Even you could not be so obtuse.'

Rafaello held her gaze for several unnerving minutes, and then, as Jaime was about to give up, he looked away. 'I do not know what you mean, *signorina*,' he declared, studying the wine in his glass. 'There can be no other reason for you to want to see me.'

Jaime's knees were knocking beneath the hem of her skirt, but she was compelled to go on: 'You must know that's not true,' she said carefully. 'After what happened——'

'After what happened—when?' he snarled angrily. 'Do you mean five years ago, when you threw my offer of marriage back in my face? Or can you possibly be referring to our confrontation six months ago, when you kindly reminded me of my responsibilities to my wife!'

'Raf——'

'No, you will hear me out! You must think I am some kind of fool, indeed. You come here, expecting to be treated in the way I would treat any other guest, when you must know that you are the last person I would wish to see.'

'Why?'

'Why?' He tossed off the rest of his brandy, and dropped the empty glass on to his desk. 'Why?' he grated. 'In God's name, Jaime, have you no shame? What manner of woman are you? What can we possibly have to say to one another, when you know in your heart that everything has been said!'

'*No!*'

'Why do you say no?' He glared at her savagely. 'What more do you want from me? What last shred of pride are you seeking here?' He lifted an unsteady hand and directed it at her. 'You told me—you told me *everything* when you said we had drunk too much wine! You did not come to Italy to help me, Jaime, you came to help Nicola make a fool of me! And now that she is dead, you come back to complete the destruction!'

'That's not true!' Jaime jerked to her feet to face him, clamping her teeth together to prevent them from chattering.

'Oh, spare me the histrionics, Jaime! I have had enough of them to last me a lifetime. Whatever your reasons for coming to Vaggio, I do not want to hear them. Nicola is dead! I am dead! And so far as I am concerned, you are dead, too!'

'No——'

The choking denial left her lips, but Rafaello was not prepared to listen to it. 'You have had a long journey,' he declared, taking a steadying breath. 'Naturally, I would not expect you to leave at this time of night. You may accept my hospitality until the morning, and then——'

'To hell with your hospitality!' burst out Jaime

tearfully, uncaring that her tears were causing her mascara to run and cause dark streaks to circle her already hollow eyes. 'I didn't come here to turn round and run away again. I came because I loved you; I came because I wanted to tell you that; I came because my life has been empty for five long years, and I hoped that now we might have a second chance!'

Rafaello was arrested as he walked towards the door, but although the sincerity of her words got through to him, their meaning didn't. 'I have had experience of your love, Jaime,' he stated harshly. 'Five years of experience, as it happens. And to my knowledge, it has never amounted to much.'

'Oh, *Raf*!' Jaime shook her head helplessly, as her last desperate plea seemed to be having no success. 'I've loved you for five years, too. Don't you think it's about time we started doing something about it?'

Rafaello's mouth curved scornfully. 'What would you suggest?' he demanded. 'Would you like me to hire an overseer so that I could spend my time in London, with you? Or would you prefer it if I sold the Castello and the vineyard, and bought a house in England? Or perhaps you have it in mind to commute from Vaggio to London, so that you could continue with your job as——'

'Stop it! Stop it!' Jaime put her hands over her ears closing her eyes against his bitter cynicism. 'You don't understand. You don't understand! I didn't come here to ask you to do any of those things. I-I came to tell you I love you. Isn't that enough?' She opened her eyes again. 'Don't you want me any more, Raf? Not even—physically?'

Rafaello's hand fell from the door handle. 'Damn

you, Jaime,' he muttered violently. 'Damn you!' His hands clenched at his sides. 'Yes, I want you. God knows, I've never stopped wanting you. But I've finally found the will to say: not on your terms!'

Jaime's hands fell to her sides. 'You don't know what my terms are.'

'I can guess.' Rafaello closed his eyes now against the unconscious appeal of drowned grey eyes and tear-wet cheeks. 'If you care about me at all, Jaime, you will get out of here, before I do something I will bitterly regret.'

'Nothing you did could be a cause of regret to me,' exclaimed Jaime, scrubbing the backs of her hands across her cheeks. 'Oh, Raf, please stop fighting me. I need you so desperately. Please—please, don't ask me to go!'

'Jaime—'

His groan of anguish came with a final bid for detachment, an unsteady groping for the handle of the door, that sent Jaime rushing across the room to him. Sobbing helplessly, she clutched at his thin waist, wrapping her arms around him and pressing her face against the finely-textured suede of his waistcoat.

'I won't let you do this, I won't!' she choked despairingly, and the yielding softness of her body against his achieved what words could not. Although his hands descended on hers cruelly, gripping her narrow wrists and digging into the flesh, they did not thrust her away. Instead, he turned rather shakenly to face her, and uttered a muffled oath of defeat as he bent his head to hers.

His mouth was hard and violent, an outlet for the starved emotions he had suppressed for so long. His hand at her nape held her a prisoner, but Jaime had no desire to resist. Her lips opened eagerly in urgent anticipation, and the kiss which had begun so savagely deepened to an aching sweetness.

When he finally released her mouth to bury his face in the scented hollow of her neck, Jaime was trembling quite uncontrollably, and his arms around her tightened possessively. 'All right,' he muttered, brokenly, 'I cannot let you go—I admit it. But if you ever leave me again, Jaime, I swear it, I will kill you!'

'I won't leave you,' promised Jaime tremulously. 'I-I didn't come here to make terms, Rafe. You're all the terms I ever wanted. Only—only I waited too long, and I thought I'd lost you for ever.'

Rafaello's brows drew together as he tipped her face up to his. 'What do you mean? You waited too long?'

'That night—that night I walked out of the hotel, I knew then I'd made a terrible mistake——'

'Yet you never came back.' Rafaello's mouth tightened.

'No.' Jaime shook her head. 'No, I didn't do that. But only because I was sure you would come after me.' She sighed. 'I was so conceited—so stubborn!' She broke off unsteadily. 'Then I read in the papers that you were going to marry Nicola, and—and there was nothing——'

'You could have stopped me!'

'What?' Jaime quivered. 'When I thought you were marrying Nicola because you wanted her?'

Rafaello was tugging the pins out of her hair, but at her words he stopped to stare into her eyes. 'I told you how it was.'

'Now you have.' Jaime nodded. 'But then—'

'*Dio mio*, Jaime, if you only knew how I hated myself that night—the night you left!' He paused. 'Tell me, if I had not—touched you, would you have forgiven me sooner?'

'Oh, Raf, there was nothing to forgive. Nothing. I didn't blame you. At least, not until you married Nicola. Then I thought——'

'—— that I had not loved you at all?'

'My mother would have said so.'

'You did not tell her?'

'No.' With her hair loose about her shoulders, Jaime looked absurdly young and vulnerable. 'My mother and I—we don't talk about things like that. We see one another perhaps twice a year, that's all.' She sighed, touching Rafaello's cheek with endearing tenderness. 'Lately,' she added, 'lately, I've been wondering whether my father was entirely to blame for what happened to their marriage. Perhaps my mother should never have got married. Maybe she never had any real feelings for either of us. In any event, I know now that I'm not like her. Living— living without you is no substitute for what we had.'

'Oh, Jaime——' Rafaello threaded the silken strands of her hair through his fingers, gathering handfuls of softness against his lips, tasting its newly-washed sweetness. 'What a lot of time we've wasted!'

'*I've* wasted,' Jaime corrected him huskily. 'Blame me, no one else.'

For a while there was silence in the study, but eventually Rafaello compelled her back from him. 'We—we have to talk,' he declared unevenly, 'and holding you like this——' He drew a deep breath. 'Well, we have to talk.'

'Can I stay?'

Jaime looked up at him anxiously, and Rafaello moved his shoulders in a helpless gesture. 'I have said so.'

'I mean—with you,' breathed Jaime, chafing at his restraining hands. 'Oh, Raf, we can talk for ever. Only now I want you to hold me.'

'Jaime, if I go on holding you——'

'I know,' she nodded. 'But why is that so wrong? It's what we both want, isn't it?'

'Jaime, I have to tell you about Nicola.'

'There's no need. I know.'

'I have to tell you that I did not know you were in ignorance about—about the child.'

'I know that, too.'

'That was why I spoke to you as I did,' he added. 'That was why I tried to hate you for taking her part.'

'Raf, it's over now.'

'Is it?' Rafaello sighed. 'I should never have married her.'

Jaime shook her head. 'Darling, she married you.'

Rafaello's hands tightened on her shoulders. 'I blamed myself at first, you know. That first child was mine. If she had not had the miscarriage——'

'Raf, you didn't cause it.' She paused. 'She told me that she—wasn't happy here. She got bored.'

Rafaello bent his head. 'I think she expected a different kind of life.'

Jaime's eyes were warm with compassion. 'Darling, didn't we all?'

Rafaello looked down at her with troubled eyes. 'I would never have left her, you know.'

'I know.' Jaime's voice broke. 'I would never have asked you to.'

'Oh, Jaime——'

With a helpless groan, Rafaello gathered her into his arms, his lips against her ear warm with the healing breath of relief. 'I love you so much,' he muttered, 'so very much. There are no words to tell you how I feel . . .'

Some hours later, Jaime awakened to find Rafaello had turned on the lamp beside his bed and was watching her as she slept. With her hair a tumbled skein of pale silk about her shoulders, and the afterglow of his lovemaking in her cheeks, she looked flushed and adorable, and Rafaello was not immune to the parted invitation of her mouth.

'Can't you sleep?' she asked drowsily, lifting her hand to stroke his cheek as he released her lips, and Rafaello smiled.

'I have all my life to sleep,' he told her, his eyes dark with emotion. 'I just wanted to assure myself that it had not all been a dream.'

'It's no dream,' Jaime whispered, linking her bare arms about his neck. 'Hmm, you look better already. I was so worried about you when I arrived.'

Rafaello's smile was wry. 'I guess I am supposed to take that as a compliment,' he remarked humorously. 'Or perhaps it is to convince me that I cannot live without you.' His eyes grew tender. 'Believe me, I need no further proof of that.'

Jaime moistened her lips. 'Will you come back to London with me? To help me clear out my apartment,' she added quickly, as his expression grew wary. 'Darling, Martin—that's my boss—Martin already knows he needs a new assistant. But I owe it to my housekeeper to explain what's going on.' She sighed. 'Poor Mrs Purdom, I don't know what she'll do.'

'You do not think she would like to live in Italy, too?' suggested Rafaello gently, his lips stroking the curve of one creamy breast. 'You will need someone to look after you, will you not? And you may be glad of an Englishwoman to take care of our children, when we have them.'

Jaime's eyes sparkled. 'Oh, Raf, what a marvellous idea!'

'I am glad you approve.' Rafaello smiled at her possessively. 'And yes, I will come with you to London. I have no intention of allowing you to leave me again, even for one night.' His lips sought hers. 'But we will come back to Vaggio for Christmas, if you can bear it.'

'It's our home,' said Jaime simply, and Rafaello bent his head in acknowledgement.

'And Nicola?'

'Perhaps she will be glad that we are happy,' said Jaime softly. 'But I'm glad you didn't share her rooms. We'll have them redecorated for visitors, for your mother.'

'My mother!' Rafaello grimaced. 'Oh, yes, I think my mother will be well pleased.'

'So do I,' murmured Jaime comfortably.

'She never wanted me to marry an English girl, you know,' he confessed, moving to imprison her beneath him. 'Until she met you. Then she changed her mind.'

'Did she?'

Jaime yielded to his demands with urgent abandonment, and as Rafaello's aroused body took possession of hers, she decided that that lady would be delighted that her plans had succeeded.

LEONARDO DA VINCI

When Jaime arrives in Rome, her plane lands at an international airport named after Leonardo da Vinci. Although da Vinci lived more than 500 years ago, he is Italy's most famous and extraordinary native son.

Born in 1452, the illegitimate son of a lawyer and a peasant girl, Leonardo was raised by his father's family in a small village near Florence. At the age of fourteen, this tall handsome youth began his apprenticeship in the Florentine studio of Verrocchio, a renowned painter. It was here that young Leonardo acquired a thirst for learning, particularly science. He also became so proficient at painting and sculpture that his ability soon outstripped Verrocchio's!

Da Vinci was to go on to become the resident artist of dukes, kings and popes, producing such great works of art as the *Last Supper* and the *Mona Lisa*. But his notebooks also reveal an incredible scientific foresight—for on the pages are elaborate diagrams for prototypes of such modern-day inventions as the airplane, the submarine and the film projector— almost as if he could see into the future.

By all accounts, da Vinci was a marvelously entertaining eccentric. He was known to have loved animals, and he liked to keep strange pets in his house. Guests would see a giant eagle flap monstrous wings and soar across the room; a porcupine might wander among the legs of guests, and a pet raven often added its squawks to lively discussions.

By the time of his death in 1519, da Vinci had been a painter, sculptor, musician, architect, map maker, astronomer, engineer, naturalist and philosopher, his revolutionary creative genius making him the quintessential Renaissance man. And considering that Leonardo da Vinci was drawing pictures of flying machines 500 years before airplanes were invented, it is more than appropriate that an airport has been named after him!

Take these
4 best-selling novels
FREE

Yes! Four sophisticated,
contemporary love stories
by four world-famous
authors of romance
FREE, as your
introduction to the Harlequin Presents
subscription plan. Thrill to **Anne Mather**'s
passionate story BORN OUT OF LOVE, set
in the Caribbean.... Travel to darkest Africa
in **Violet Winspear**'s TIME OF THE TEMPTRESS....Let
Charlotte Lamb take you to the fascinating world of London's
Fleet Street in MAN'S WORLD .... Discover beautiful Greece in
Sally Wentworth's moving romance SAY HELLO TO YESTERDAY.

Harlequin Presents...

*The very finest
in romance fiction*

Join the millions of avid Harlequin readers all over the
world who delight in the magic of a really exciting novel.
EIGHT great NEW titles published EACH MONTH!
Each month you will get to know exciting, interesting,
true-to-life people .... You'll be swept to distant lands you've
dreamed of visiting .... Intrigue, adventure, romance, and
the destiny of many lives will thrill you through each
Harlequin Presents novel.

Get all the latest books before they're sold out!
As a Harlequin subscriber you actually receive your
personal copies of the latest Presents novels immediately
after they come off the press, so you're sure of getting all
8 each month.

Cancel your subscription whenever you wish!
You don't have to buy any minimum number of books.
Whenever you decide to stop your subscription just let us
know and we'll cancel all further shipments.